NEVER SAY YOU NEED ME

TRINITY LAKES ROMANCE
BOOK EIGHTEEN

AMANDA DEED

FREE inDEED MEDiA

FREE inDEED MEDIA

Never Say You Need Me

A Trinity Lakes Romance

Published by Free inDeed Media, 2025

www.freeindeedmedia.com

© Amanda deed 2025

Cover design by Annie Millard

ISBN 978-0-6458404-5-2 (e-book)

ISBN 978-0-6458404-4-5 (paperback)

CHAPTER ONE

Amelia Jones hovered her finger over the delete button of her dating profile and groaned. What was she doing? Why had she even set it up in the first place? A year ago, she would have scorned anyone who suggested she should sign up to a match-making site. A year ago, she'd sworn off men, convinced they weren't worth her time. A year ago, she believed an independent life was all she wanted.

But Nick Gordon and Mud Murchison arrived in Trinity Lakes and upended all her beliefs, or misbeliefs, whichever the case may be. And now, very little satisfied her expectations. Expectations she was unclear about. Seriously, confusion made her second-guess everything of late. None of the online dates she'd met struck her as anything more than self-centered, egotistical, or one-thing-on-their-mind kinds of guys. Sure, a couple had been super good-looking, but that wasn't enough.

One minute she was over all men forever—never wanted to be coupled with one again—and the next minute, it was as if her eyes suddenly opened to a new possibility. A new hope.

And now her brain, or perhaps her heart, refused to shut it down again.

The thing that opened her eyes? Mud—Mike Murchison. So free. So full of adventure. Not tied down to responsibilities. Not needing anyone. Untethered. Unencumbered. Unhindered. The lifestyle Amelia secretly dreamed of year in and year out.

And then to top it off, watching the way Nick Gordon—Mud's best friend—loved and treated Violet, woke a desire in her for the same. Amelia sighed. She had gone to church with Violet and Nick a few times, hoping to meet someone, but all were spoken for. Or didn't appeal to her at all.

With a grunt, she hit the button that would confirm her cancellation and shoved the tablet away from her. She rose and stood by the large windows that overlooked the lakes in the valley, which were shrouded in morning mist. Why wouldn't this restlessness leave her? For a time, she'd found contentment in her work with Violet and their circle of friends. But lately, all those dreams of finding her match had surfaced and churned constantly within. Would she never find someone to love her? Would she live out her days as a lonely administrative assistant?

She opened and closed her fists. *Stop it, Amelia. Stop living in this fantasy. You are such a fool.*

She pushed her thoughts aside with a frustrated groan and returned to her desk. After all, she was supposed to be working, looking after the office work while Violet and Nick were away in some exotic location, enjoying the sun and each other.

Amelia groaned again. Why couldn't she be happy for them? They were on a business jaunt to discover ways to help families in Africa. It's not like they were on their honeymoon, bathing in the sun. Their wedding was still a couple of months away. More likely they were in the hot, dusty desert, battling flies and heat to reach those most in need. When had she become so resentful?

She needed to get over this. How was she supposed to be Violet's maid of honor with envy attacking her all the time? Especially when she'd have to spend time with Mud as Nick's best man.

Amelia dropped her head into her hands. Mud. Shorter than average, but every inch gorgeous, solid brawn and endless energy. She'd developed a massive infatuation for him, even in the few weeks he visited. But he'd only had eyes for her friend, Breanna. Not the shy, bookish office girl, always in the background, always invisible to those she wanted to see her most. An image came to mind of Donkey, jumping up and down in the movie, *Shrek*, crying "Pick me. Pick me."

At least she wouldn't have to deal with Mud for a couple of months. He wasn't due to appear until two weeks before the big wedding. Thank goodness for small mercies. He was to blame for her phase of emotional upheaval, after all. Amelia straightened in her ergonomic chair and forced her attention to the work at hand.

But trying to concentrate wouldn't cut it today. Just before lunchtime, she changed into the active wear she always kept in her car and drove down to Lake Wainscott to go for a run along the shore. She hooked earbuds over her ears to listen to one of her favorite Georgette Heyer novels as she jogged. Listening to a book would help drown out her more depressing thoughts.

It seemed to work. After some cooling down stretches and feeling more energized and in control, Amelia stopped at Becky's Coffee Cart. She wanted to grab a coffee and a sandwich before heading back to the office.

"How are things?" Becky asked as she steamed the milk for Amelia's mocha.

"Not too bad." She didn't want to give the woman a rundown of her thoughts for the day.

"I still can't get over Nick and Violet. What a surprise. But such a great couple."

Amelia groaned on the inside. She couldn't escape them, even when they weren't in town. "Yes, they are." She tried not to sigh. Of course, the announcement hadn't been a surprise at all for those close to Violet last summer.

"I bet it's going to be a big, flash wedding."

"No," Amelia said. "Neither of them are into that. They're keeping it simple. Although, simple will still look amazing to the rest of us. Especially if Mr. Reynolds gets his way."

She'd seen Violet roll her eyes several times when relaying conversations with her father. He wanted the biggest and the best for his daughter. Amelia figured the reality would land somewhere between the glamorous splurge of his wishes and the barefooted beachside function of Violet's. Amelia wasn't sure on which side Nick's preferences lay. He seemed too busy, lost in Violet's eyes half the time.

"Any inside news on the wedding dress?" Becky winked at her.

Amelia smiled in return and made a gesture across her lips. "Sworn to secrecy, I'm afraid." The girls would sigh over the understated satin gown that hugged Violet's figure before flaring out into a small train. The very image of an elegant mermaid. Amelia's dress and that of the other bridesmaids were of a similar shape in a dusty blue color, only without the train.

"Well, I can only try." Becky shrugged as she handed Amelia her coffee.

Still enjoying the late fall sunshine, Amelia waved goodbye to Becky and headed to a park bench to eat. The office work would still be there when she returned. No hurry.

The talk of weddings with Becky brought back Amelia's nostalgia. She opened her phone and went to the browser, scrolling through images of wedding dresses. When ... *if* ... it was her turn, she would wear something that reminded her of her favorite fairy tales. Big, wide skirts, lots of lace, and probably a splash of color for extra zing.

Amelia sighed and put her phone down. She was dreaming. It would never happen. And she wasn't even sure she wanted it to. She took a bite out of her sandwich and watched the bird life playing in the water at the edge of the lake. She tore pieces of crust and tossed them to the ducks, who scrambled to snatch the crumbs.

A few minutes later, her phone pinged with a text from Violet.

Where are you?

Amelia pressed her lips together. When would she catch a break? She shook her head. What was her problem? This was her best friend and workmate.

Having lunch down by the lake. What's up?

The answer came back quickly.

I need you to go back to the office.

Sure. I'll just finish my sandwich and head back.

Sorry, but can you go now?

Amelia turned her phone face down on her knee with an inward groan. Violet wasn't usually this pushy. But Amelia wasn't usually this resistant. She sighed and rose from the bench, tucking her half-eaten lunch into her bag.

OK. On my way. What's the problem?

No reply came. Either business had interrupted Violet—a

likely scenario—or she was waiting for Amelia to get back before continuing the conversation. Whichever was the case, Amelia now sat in the driver's seat on her way to the estate on the hill and couldn't check her phone until she arrived. Unless, of course, Violet called.

As she drove along Main Street, the lights for the pedestrian crossing turned yellow and she shifted her foot to the brake. The car in front of her kept driving. A chill spread up Amelia's spine as she saw a teenager, phone in hand, step into the road. Seconds split into increments and slowed as the car in front of her struck the boy and he fell to the road, unmoving. Amelia screamed in horror and pulled her car to a stop. She put the hazard lights on, quickly unbuckling and almost falling out of the car in her haste.

The driver ahead of her didn't stop but continued on out of town. With her heart thudding like a war drum in her ears, Amelia hurried to the young man sprawled on the ground. Blood oozed from his head where it had met with the pavement. One of his arms sat at a gruesome angle. What to do? What to do? Her mind scrambled, trying to recall any first aid training she'd received, but her brain refused to comply.

Others gathered around, and at last their voices forged their way through the fog in her head. "Call 911!"

Amelia looked at the phone that hung in her limp hand. 911. 911. *Call 911.*

———

MIKE MURCHISON, known to all and sundry as Mud, sat on the porch step of Violet Reynold's house in the country club estate, and typed a brief text message to his friend Nick Gordon.

Bro, where are you?

He'd had the taxi driver drop him at Violet's assuming he'd find one or the other of them here. Sure, this was a surprise visit, but Nick must be somewhere close by.

His phone pinged as an answer came through.

In Africa. LOL. I told you that weeks ago. How's the mountain biking with Griff?

Mud rubbed a hand over his face. Had Nick told him that? Maybe. Probably went in one ear and out the other. But what was he supposed to say now? "Hey, my brother just died, so ..."

He swallowed the lump of emotion that rose. No, he wouldn't drop that bomb over the phone or via text message. Nick would wonder why Mud was in Trinity Lakes so early, though. The original plan was to travel with his brother for a bit, and then come to the Lakes for Nick's wedding. But no, that plan came crashing down, along with Griff's mountain bike on Whistler.

Trip cut short. I'm in Trinity Lakes, at Vi's actually. Forgot you were away. He didn't want Nick to worry or press him for information, so added, *All Good.*

Minutes ticked by with no response and Mud stood up to pace the driveway. He refused to dwell on his grief. He just wanted to be around great friends and have a good time, that's all he needed. Hanging out with Nick would ease his anguish, surely. Except he wasn't here.

The hard-rock rhythm of his ringtone startled him. Nick.

"Yeah?" Mud answered.

"Dude. Sorry. I know you've just got there, and we'll talk later, but we need your help, urgently."

Mud's whole body came alive at the alarm in Nick's voice. "What's up?"

"Amelia's been involved in an accident and needs help getting her car sorted."

Mud's stomach twisted in all kinds of knots. Why him? Why now? To rescue a damsel in distress wasn't at the top of his to-do list. In fact, it didn't get a mention on any list of priorities. Wasn't there anyone else to help her? "But—"

"I'll owe you big time. We'd just asked her to head back there, knowing you were on your own. Vi's booking you an Uber as we speak." Nick was clearly worried.

"Okay. Sure."

Mud ended the call shortly after and groaned, scratching his head in frustration. What he wouldn't give for an evening at a club, dancing, drinking and forgetting it all. Or a full-on workout at the gym with deafening music to drown out his thoughts. Surely, if he took off now, Amelia would be fine.

Another groan escaped him as he realized he'd never go through with such a cowardly, heartless act. A few years as a firefighter had trained him to run toward trouble, not turn tail and fly the other way. Besides, the Uber pulled into the driveway even now. Mud clamped down on the internal storm which raged. He'd better do the right thing. Especially since it seemed Amelia got into an accident on account of his surprise arrival.

"To Main Street please, near the Bellbird Cafe will be fine." He slid into the back seat.

Nick hadn't given Mud much information, except to find Amelia and drive her car back. That's all he knew. But as they pulled into Main Street, Mud realized it might be serious. Traffic stood still and flashing lights filled his vision—both ambulance and police—and his stomach knotted even more.

He paid the driver as images of his brother's broken body flashed through his mind, and he turned away from the scene. He couldn't look. Didn't want to face what happened here and now, nor the memories that burned so fresh.

Mud's heartbeat ratcheted, and his breath came quickly. *No. Not now.* He wiped his slick hands down his jeans and sat on the nearest bench. *Deep breaths, Mud.* In through the nose —two, three, four—and out through the mouth, two, three, four, five, six, seven.

He punched his fist into his thigh. *Come on, man.* It wasn't like he'd never been in this situation before. It had been one tragedy and trauma after another of late. *Stop being a loser and get up.*

Mud forced himself to his feet, turned to survey the scene before him and trudged towards the accident. His eyes landed first on a tarp over an inert figure on the road, with both cops and paramedics standing around. The fact they seemed inactive spoke reams. Someone had died. *Oh no.* Was it Amelia? No, Nick said she needed help, nothing more.

One trooper worked with cordon tape, stringing it up to keep the sticky beaks away, although several people stood nearby with their phones held up, capturing the scene on video. Mud shook his head. Why did people care more about their social content than showing compassion in these situations? It grated on him. Like it always had at every fire he'd attended. Every road accident. Every tragedy.

His irritation gave him motivation to move forward, find Amelia, and get her out of there. Several meters away, a woman sat at the back of an ambulance, with a paramedic and an officer speaking to her. Was that Amelia?

Mud moved closer only to find an arm stretched across his chest, barring his progress.

"Sorry, sir. You can't come through."

He swerved his gaze to the state trooper who held him back and gritted back an ugly retort. "I'm here to collect

Amelia Jones." He gestured toward the ambulance. Hopefully he pointed to the right person. As yet, he hadn't seen her face to be certain.

The officer turned away slightly, spoke into his radio, and then looked back at him. "Name?"

"Mike Murchison."

The constable relayed his name.

"Or Mud. She probably knows me as Mud. My nickname." He probably sounded a little stupid explaining.

Again, the trooper repeated the information and after a pause, waved Mud through toward the ambulance.

"Thanks, mate." Mud nodded as he shouldered past him, keeping his eyes diverted from the ominous tarp.

As he approached the ambulance, his movement must have caught Amelia's attention, for her chin lifted toward him and she squinted into the sunshine. "You?" Then she shuddered.

Shuddered? That was the effect of shock, surely. And forget the fact her face was as pale as the white sand on most Australian beaches, what was that tone in her voice? "Yeah, it's me. I arrived early for the wedding." He shrugged and shoved his hands in his pockets.

"But what are you doing *here*?"

Okay, he would definitely put that question down to shock. "I'm here to drive you home." He shifted his gaze to the paramedic. "That is, if she's ready?"

"Well, she is suffering from shock, so—"

"Keep her safe, warm, and hydrated." Mud finished for him. "Yep. I've got it."

He'd got it down to a fine art after seeing plenty of people with shock, and his own experience two weeks ago. This wouldn't be as simple as "drive her home." *Thank you, Nick.* He'd have to stay with Amelia tonight and make sure she was okay. He let out a huff, realizing he'd been too abrupt. "Sorry. I'm a firefighter. I'm aware of the attention required."

"Right." The paramedic nodded. "Well, she's witnessed a terrible accident, so go easy." He helped Amelia to her feet, tucking the thermal sheet around her shoulders.

Mud pressed his lips together. As if he'd be callous toward someone clearly traumatized.

Another official-looking man in uniform stepped up. "Ms. Jones?" He looked at Amelia.

"Y…yes." She still shivered.

"I'm Sheriff Thompson." He held out a business card. "When you're up to it, I'll need you to come to the station and give us a statement."

Mud took the card when Amelia merely nodded. "I'll make sure she does." Then he closed his eyes, mentally scolding himself. Why'd he make that promise? Seriously.

"The sooner, the better," the Sheriff added in a low tone so only Mud could hear. "We want to catch the driver before they disappear."

"Absolutely." Mud gave him a firm nod, then moved to Amelia's side to escort her away from the scene. "Let's get you home." He scanned the street. "Umm, which is your car?"

"Oh." Amelia shook her head as though trying to dislodge something. Then she pointed. "That one, there."

Mud followed her gaze and lifted his brows. A dark green Mini Cooper. Cute. "Alrighty. Keys?" He held out his hand.

"Umm." Amelia's arms moved beneath the thermal sheet as she checked her pockets, then shook her head. "I don't know."

"Did you leave them in the car?" Mud asked, guiding her over there. Probably, amid the chaos, she left everything without a second thought, which would be completely understandable. He shaded his eyes and peered into the car.

Yep. There they were, in the cup holder. "Found them." He offered Amelia a grin, trying to minimize her stress, then guided her around to the passenger side. He made sure she was secure before heading back to the driver's side.

"Now. Where's home?" Mud asked once he had fastened his seatbelt and started the car. He'd been to Vi's home and Breanna's last year, but that was it.

"Oh." She frowned and rubbed her forehead, then finally mumbled an address. He activated the car's navigation system and entered what she'd told him. No sense asking her to give directions. She was as vague as a misty mountain road right now.

The troopers moved cordons and waved him out of the accident zone. Within ten minutes they'd arrived at her little unit. Once again, he skirted the car to help her out and guide her inside, using her keys to unlock the door. Perhaps this was a good thing, because looking after her right now kept his mind off his own trauma.

"Okay. Why don't you sit down, and I'll get you a blanket and make you a hot cuppa," he told her. "How does that sound?"

Amelia lifted her pale face to his, her brows furrowed. "You don't have to stay. Don't you want to see Bree?"

CHAPTER TWO

At Amelia's mention of Breanna, Mud stood stock still for a second, but then shook his head. "You're what's important right now. You've suffered a major shock, and we need to make sure you're okay."

"I'm fine." The last thing Amelia wanted was to seem helpless. Even though the kindness in his eyes was so very welcome. If only she could stop this darned shivering.

Within seconds, Mud had grabbed the quilt from her bed and draped it over her. "Now, did you say coffee, tea or hot chocolate?"

What was it she liked to drink again? Every thought seemed to slur in her brain, like the lag on an old computer. "Oh, umm, I have some hot chocolate packets, I think." She waved a hand toward the small kitchen.

Numb. That's what she felt. Like everything moved in slow motion since that awful ...

No, she didn't want to remember that. The troopers tried to coax all the details from her, but she couldn't even remember the car. *Ugh. Stop thinking, girl.* She needed to watch a movie to keep her mind occupied. Amelia lifted the blanket off and was about to collect the remote when Mud re-entered the room.

"No, you don't," he commanded. He placed two mugs on the coffee table and tucked her back in.

"I was just turning the TV on," she complained. What? Did he suppose she was heading out for her daily jog or something?

He grinned at her. "Oh, sorry. I thought you might be off to run around the block."

Wait. What? Did he read her mind?

"Are you okay?" He must have seen the shock in her face, because his gaze became intense.

"Yeah, I'm okay." She leaned forward to pick up her mug. *But please don't ask me about the accident.*

She breathed a quiet sigh of relief when he sat down beside her with the remote, opened the streaming service, and started scrolling through movie options. "Hmm, no." He advanced past several action movies and crime thrillers. "Only Disney fairy tales for you today." He landed on the old, animated version of *Beauty and the Beast.* "How's this?"

Amelia's insides did a flip-flop. "My favorite." How did he know?

He leaned closer with a conspiratorial whisper. "Don't tell anyone. It's one of my favorites, too."

Amelia couldn't help but giggle, although she covered her mouth with her hand. "What? How?"

Mud screwed up his face. "Were you aware Nick has three sisters? They played these movies repeatedly when we were teens." He rolled his eyes and grinned. "But, I mean, they are great, really, aren't they?" He launched into the song about Gaston with as much gusto as the movie itself, then did a perfect impersonation of Lumiere.

Amelia laughed again. Mud's theatrical skills were brilliant. To be honest, she was a little awe-struck, but she didn't want him to know it. "Shhh. It's starting." She waved a hand at him.

For the next hour they sat sipping drinks and nibbling popcorn Mud had scrounged from her pantry, but watched the film in silence. Except for when he sang along to the music or joined in speaking the characters' lines.

But near the end, right when Belle wept over the Beast thinking he was dead, Amelia's emotions suddenly came back to life in a rush. So strong was the wave that she gasped. "I can't breathe. I can't breathe." Heaving sobs burst from her.

"Hey, hey, hey," Mud said in a soothing voice. He immediately paused the video and shifted closer to her, putting a reassuring hand on her back. "It's okay. Do you want to talk about it?"

Did she want to? Yes. But to this guy who likely didn't give a straw for her emotional state? Definitely not.

She'd lost her ability to articulate, anyway. Though she'd buried her face in the blanket, she shook her head. The trauma of the day had finally hit home, and it refused to be held back. She'd thought that boy was dead.

Once again, Mud impressed her with the steady presence of his hand on her back. Then he pressed a bunch of tissues into her hand, which she quickly used to blow her nose.

Great. Now he was going to see her ugly, puffy eyes and snotty sobbing. Too bad. Memories of the moment of impact between the car ahead of her and the boy flooded in. The sickening thud. The blood. The grotesque shapes.

Shapes plural. There were two. There'd been a dog.

Amelia jerked her head up. "Do you know what happened to the dog?"

Mud frowned. "What dog?"

"The kid was walking a dog. I didn't see it until after I got out of my car. They were both lying there. I saw them take the boy off to hospital, but was the dog alright?"

"Umm," Mud stuttered. "I … I saw a tarp over a body. I thought …" He cleared his throat and swallowed. "I thought that was the victim of the hit and run—the boy, as you say." He paused. "I guess it was the dog I saw. I assume it died."

Well, that was enough to send her off into another fit of tears. The thought of an innocent pet being run over and killed by a careless driver saddened her. Or was it relief that the boy might be ok? Probably both. "Did you hear anything about the boy?" she mumbled into her hands.

"Not a thing. Sorry." Mud's voice was hushed. "Try not to worry about it all now. You need to rest. These kinds of traumas … they can take it out of you. There's time enough to go over it all tomorrow."

———

AMELIA DRIED her eyes again and looked at him. What was it about him? It was as though he knew what he was talking about? Like, *really* knew. She nodded, acknowledging his advice.

"You probably should eat something." He slapped his hands on his thighs and stood. "I'm not much of a cook, but I can rustle up something simple." He started walking to the kitchen.

"I think I have a few packets of ramen noodles, but I can do it." She tossed the blanket aside. She wasn't injured and didn't need him waiting on her hand and foot.

"No, you don't." Mud turned and motioned for her to stay. "You stay there and rest."

Truth be told, when she stood her knees still wobbled. She probably should stay on the sofa after all.

Mud busied himself in the kitchen, occasionally asking her where utensils lived, but he'd started whistling while he worked. No tune she recognized, but it was a pleasant sound, a little calming, if she was honest. He brought her another cup of hot cocoa while the noodles simmered and, on his way back to the kitchen, his pocket started roaring with a classic rock tune.

He pulled his phone out and answered. "Hey Nick."

Nick's voice was inaudible on the other end of the call, but Amelia assumed it would be a checkup. Sure enough, Mud's next words confirmed it.

"Yeah, she's okay. Just in shock. She witnessed a hit and run."

This started questions in Amelia's mind. How had Mud known to pick her up? How did Nick find out something was up? Amelia must have called Vi straight after the accident—not that she remembered—it was all still fuzzy in her head. She rubbed her face again.

"Well, I was going to stay with you, dude, but you're not here."

Amelia tuned in to the one-sided conversation again. What had she missed? The fact that Mud turned his back to her and lowered his voice didn't help.

"It's fine. She shouldn't be left alone anyway."

Silence for a moment.

"Dude, she's not even my type. Nothing's going to happen. I'm just monitoring her until she gets over the worst of this shock."

Was Mud talking about staying with her for the night? But the words "not my type" overran every other thought in her head. Yeah, that about summed it up. He'd never noticed her last year when she was practically falling at his feet. And now he was only here to play doctor. As soon as she was well, he would be gone. Probably back to poor Bree. As if Amelia expected anything else.

Had she expected anything else? He was still as cute as ever, and having him doting on her made her insides quiver. Unless that was just the shock. Yes, that must be it. Because sure as heck, she wouldn't fall for him again. Especially knowing his interest in her bottomed out at less than zero. And especially remembering how he'd ghosted Bree after he left America last year.

———

"WHEN ARE YOU COMING BACK, ANYWAY?" Mud asked Nick. In a time when he needed his friend more than ever, he was unavailable.

"We're helping an orphanage, but we should be back in another week. How come you're not in Canada mountain biking with Griff anymore."

Mud swallowed at the mention of his brother's name. "He, ah …" No. He refused to tell Nick over the phone. "Something came up and he couldn't continue." He quickly shifted gear. "So I came here to hang out with you until the wedding."

"Okay, well, sorry I'm not there. I'm happy for you to stay at my place, but I'll have to contact my flat mate to let you in."

"All good. Like I said, I'm right for tonight."

"Well, I'll have it sorted for tomorrow. I'll send you the address and Manny's phone number, but don't call him until I've cleared it with him. I'll let you know. Okay?"

"Yeah. Ta. Appreciate it."

They said their goodbyes and Mud ended the call. After adding the seasoning mix to the noodles, he served them into two bowls and headed back to Amelia, who still appeared a little pale.

"How are you doing?" He asked her, handing her a bowl. Her sense of numbness, the sensation he was so familiar with, was obviously wearing off.

"You don't need to stay here, you know."

So bristly. She must have overheard him on the phone despite keeping his voice down. Mud remembered what he'd said about her and groaned internally. *What an idiot.* He drew in a breath and forced a smile. "But I'm staying anyway. Shock is hard, and this couch is comfy as. All I need is a blanket. You got a spare?"

"I'm fine." Amelia pressed her lips together.

"No, you're not fine." Mud argued and sat back with his food, waving his fork at her. "Eat your noodles."

Amelia stared at him. Daggers, if he were to guess. But he ignored her and turned back to the TV, pressing play to watch the end of *Beauty and the Beast*. Her fork soon clinked on the ceramic bowl as she ate. Good girl.

By the time they'd eaten, the credits of the movie were rolling. Mud collected the dishes and headed for the kitchen once again. "Do you want to watch another movie?"

Amelia rubbed her face. "No. I'm getting pretty tired. I'll probably take a shower and go to bed."

Mud put the dishes in the sink and watched her get up, still shaky. "You right? You need help?"

She glared at him. "Don't think you're following me into the bathroom."

"As if." Mud rolled his eyes, but did a double take as he saw hurt flash across her face. "I mean, I'm sure you're very attractive and everything, but that's not what I'm here for."

"Wow." She gaped at him then stalked off to the bathroom, throwing words over her shoulder. "Blankets are in the linen closet along with a towel if you need one later. I'll see you in the morning if you're still here."

Mud sank onto the couch, which still had the quilt from her bed on it. He should probably take it into her room while she was in the shower, lest he get himself in trouble again. Yikes, he was messing this up. *Way to make her feel like trash, Mud.* And it wasn't like she was unattractive at all. Quite the opposite, in fact. Why he hadn't noticed her last year, he couldn't fathom.

When he said to Nick she wasn't his type, it was more about her quiet personality, not about how she looked. She was wearing active gear when he picked her up this afternoon and man, how it showed off her figure. And apart from the ashen look on her face, she was really pretty. Gorgeous in fact. But he'd only ever gone out with party girls. All fun and nothing serious.

Maybe that should change. Maybe he should look for someone more settled in life. He ran a hand through his hair. What was he thinking? This was grief talking. Surely. Not a good time to make any kind of life decisions. No. Tomorrow, he would hit the gym hard and go out clubbing, even if he had to drive a hundred miles to find one. Back to his normal routine. That's what he needed. Especially since Nick wasn't around. He hoped Breanna would be up for a night out.

With a plan settled in his mind, Mud set about cleaning up their evening's dishes. When Amelia's bedroom door finally clicked shut, he headed to the shower. Not that he had fresh clothes to wear, as he'd left all his luggage at the front of Violet's house. Hopefully, it would still be there tomorrow.

The morning came around too soon, it seemed, with the

sound of the coffee pot brewing in the kitchen. Mud sat up and quickly pulled on his jeans before Amelia chanced to see him in his boxers. Thankfully, she had her back turned to him as she pottered around.

"How are you this morning?" he asked as he pulled his T-shirt over his head.

"Much better, thank you," she answered. "I think the sleep helped a lot. Coffee?"

"Great. Thanks." Mud shoved his hands in his pockets. "Hey, I'm sorry if I made you uncomfortable last night."

Amelia shrugged. "I was in a state. It's all good." She handed him a steaming cup. "I was totally useless in that accident. Like, I completely froze." She shuddered.

Mud nodded. "Don't be too hard on yourself. Plenty of people are the same. Trauma affects different people in different ways."

"Thank you. But I was difficult last night, you can admit it."

Mud released a gentle laugh. "Trust me, I've seen worse." When she seemed confused, he elaborated. "I worked as a firefighter back in Australia."

"Oh. Of course. That makes sense." She sipped at her drink. "What do you have planned for today?"

She really wanted to be rid of him, didn't she? He sighed. "Well, I need to collect my luggage from Vi's place—"

"I can give you a lift since I work there," Amelia interrupted.

"Um, I reckon you should take the day off," Mud advised her. "You might still suffer some after-shocks."

Amelia gave him a tight-lipped smile at his pun. "I'm fine."

"I'm sure you are, but give yourself a break, yeah? Don't put too much pressure on yourself. I'm sure Vi will understand."

She pressed her lips together and he suspected she was ready to argue further.

"Look, these things can sneak up on you. It's better to be home where you feel safe. Besides, it's Saturday."

Amelia let out a long breath. "Okay. Sure." She took another sip. "You might as well use my car if I'm not going anywhere."

Mud lifted his eyebrows. That was unexpected. "That would be great. Are you sure?"

She shrugged. "No biggie."

"Well, that means I can sort out where I'm staying as well."

"Yes. Do whatever you need to do."

As long as it meant he was out of her hair. He got it. "I'll give you my number. Call me if you need anything."

After throwing down a piece of toast that screamed for Vegemite, he grabbed Amelia's keys and headed out. He wasn't used to jelly as a topping for toast, but rather than offending Amelia, he ate it. But he stopped at the Bell Bird Cafe as he passed through town for something a little more substantial.

His stomach relieved with a meat pie, Mud collected his luggage from Violet's house. Then he made his way to the address Nick had sent him, along with instructions on where to find a spare key. Thank goodness he could finally get out of his traveling clothes and freshen up.

Back in Amelia's car, he drove around to Breanna's flat. Would she be happy to see him again? It wasn't as though they had been serious or anything, just some fun companionship while he was in the States last year. The type of fun companionship he needed now. Especially with Nick not around to keep him occupied.

He jogged to the front door and knocked, nervous energy coursing through him.

"Amelia, what—" The door swung open with Bree's words that halted on sight of him. "What are *you* doing here?"

Bree looked past him to Amelia's car. "I thought it was Amelia."

"Nah. I'm driving her car. It's great to see you, Bree."

She stood there with the door still half open, face clouded with surprise and possible wariness. "What do you want?"

"Umm." He cleared his throat. Not the welcome he was hoping for. "I was wondering if you'd like to hang out again. Like tonight?"

Bree folded her arms across her chest. "Not a phone call, not even a text message, and you think, what, that you can just pick up where we left off?"

Mud let out a short breath. "I thought we both agreed it wasn't serious. We were having fun, weren't we?" Suddenly, he wasn't so sure. Had she hoped for more? Why did girls always take him more seriously than he ever expected them to?

Bree shook her head. "You were having fun, sure." She looked aside and mumbled. "And maybe I was, for a while."

"But?" He recognized the unuttered word hanging between them.

She shrugged. "It doesn't matter." Still, she avoided eye contact. "Anyway, I've moved on. I am seeing someone else. So, no, I won't be coming out with you tonight." With those words, she shut the door in his face.

CHAPTER THREE

A melia sat on her sofa, chewing her lip after finishing a call with Breanna who'd called and given her an earful. Why hadn't she discouraged Mud from going around there? Why hadn't she told Mud that Bree had a boyfriend? She might have, at the very least, given Bree a warning.

Amelia didn't have any answers for her. Truth was, she wanted Mud to face that problem directly and get a dose of his own treatment. Poor Bree had been heartbroken after he left for Australia and never contacted her. It didn't matter that he made no promises to her, or that she understood all along he would leave. In her heart, Breanna had tied herself to him and the rift had been agonizing.

Amelia, Violet and Lucy had consoled Bree over and over. Nick and Vi had refused to get involved, although she suspected Nick had spoken with Mud on the issue several times with no luck. Mud didn't want to be tied down. It was something Amelia admired and abhorred at the same time.

Admired because she had always yearned for that kind of freedom. After Mom left and Pa got sick, Amelia had to care for him day in and day out. Then she watched him die slowly, not being able to motivate him to fight, while waiting on him hand and foot. When he finally passed away, a sense of relief filled her, but that brought incredible grief. She was a horrible daughter.

And perhaps that's what made Mud's lifestyle seem abhorrent as well—because the pain he left in his wake could well be the pain she might leave in her wake if she acted the same. Years of being tied to her father made the thought of again being needed in such an intense way unbearable. Like, it physically made her feel sick.

Neither did she want to come across to anyone as needy. Unfortunately, yesterday's accident showed how vulnerable she could be. She clenched her hands in her lap. She didn't want to lean on anyone. Ever.

Though right now, she was almost desperate for company—someone to take her mind off this mess and keep her busy. With Violet away and Mud ordering her to stay home, the images of yesterday kept flashing through her mind.

Violet had told her repeatedly that Jesus was the way to find strength and comfort and provision. But Amelia didn't need a crutch. How annoying and draining it must be for God with everyone begging and pleading for His help all the time. Surely, He would be like "toughen up, kiddo," or "suck it up, princess." Well, that was how Pa had acted when she showed any weakness.

Funny how Mud was exactly the opposite yesterday. Even the memory of his compassion filled her with warmth and discomfort at the same time. She couldn't let him close. It would be too easy to fall for him again. And that would spell disaster in capital letters, because she was certain he would up and leave as soon as Nick and Vi's wedding was done.

A knock came at the front door, and she frowned. Violet wasn't due back yet, so who could it be? Bree had said her piece over the phone, so she doubted her friend would come around to continue her confrontation face to face. Amelia swung open the door.

Mud. Great.

"Hey." He greeted with a half-smile. "Just bringing your car back."

Amelia turned back inside. "You have a key. Why didn't you let yourself in?"

Mud followed her. "Well, I thought that would be impolite. I didn't want to intrude."

She returned to the sofa where she had been sitting. "How are you going to get yourself around?"

"I've organized a hire car, which I'll pick up later."

Oh, he must mean a rental car. "Of course." What a dumb question. She changed tack. "Bree called me."

Mud paused. Stock still. "She did?"

"Yes." She peered up at him. "She's not happy."

"Yeah, I got that." He folded his arms across his chest.

"With me either."

At that, his eyes widened. "Why? You didn't do anything?"

Amelia sighed. "Exactly. Apparently, I should have told you to stay away from her."

"Sorry I got you into trouble."

"You broke her heart." Amelia murmured the words to her folded hands which rested in her lap.

Mud was silent for a breath. "I'm starting to see." He swallowed. "I ..."

"What?"

He cleared his throat and straightened his shoulders. "Never mind. How's the shock going today?"

Way to change the subject. Amelia chanced a look at him

but saw genuine concern in his expression. She shrugged. "I'm antsy. I don't want to dwell on it, but I don't know what to do with myself."

Mud nodded like he understood. "Sometimes, when I get like that, I go to the gym. I find a good workout helps to expel the energy."

"That sounds good. I might try that." Hadn't she gone for a run yesterday for the same reason?

"I was going to go this arvo if you want."

"The Sarvo?" Amelia quirked her brow. "Is that the name of the gym?"

Mud chuckled. "This afternoon." He articulated each word carefully. "You can join me if you like."

Amelia smirked at him. "No need to be condescending with all your Aussie lingo. But it sounds like you're fishing for a ride."

"Was it that obvious?" Mud rolled his eyes good-naturedly.

Ten minutes later, Amelia slid behind the wheel of her car, Mud beside her, but as soon as she started the engine, her hands became slick and panic rose. "I can't." Her breath came quickly as she looked across at Mud. "I can't drive."

"Hey, hey, hey." He grabbed her right hand and held tight. "It's okay. You witnessed something terrible yesterday. It can take time to get back to normal."

The pressure on Amelia's hand centered her, brought calm. She nodded, trying to slow her breathing.

"I can drive if you want."

Amelia nodded again and scrambled out of the driver's seat. But she found, even as a passenger, her heart skipped a beat every time he braked, at every intersection, at the sight of anyone on the footpath. For pity's sake. How had she turned into such a wimpy mess? She tried to focus on her breathing as Mud had coached her. Even attempted to focus on social media on her phone, but her eyes wouldn't stay on the screen. By the time they got to the gym, she was genuinely sorry for Mud. He probably had fingernail marks in his arms from where she had grabbed him a few times.

"I'm sorry, Mud," she said as she got out of the car, relief blowing through her like a breeze. "This is so not me."

"It's fine. I completely understand." He even grinned at her, but not mockingly. Rather, in an I-get-it kind of way. Had he been through some trauma himself?

Amelia kept a surreptitious eye on him while she jogged on the treadmill, a narrator reading the words of Georgette Heyer through her ear buds. He was working hard. Like, *really* hard. He pushed weights she would never dream of with what looked like agony straining his face and neck. Was that grimace merely about the pain of muscle burn? Or something else? He'd said he liked to go to the gym to work off steam, so what kind of steam was he talking about? Perhaps his encounter with an angry Breanna that morning. Maybe frustration at being stuck with Amelia. Whatever it was, it seemed pretty serious. Would she be game to ask him about it later?

Whenever Mud's gaze shifted her way, she looked down at the controls on her machine and pretended to analyze or adjust. No way he was going to become aware of her interest. Well, interest might be overstating it. Call it curiosity, that was enough to acknowledge. Even if seeing his biceps and quads in high definition stirred that old attraction again, making it hard to look away.

One thing was for sure. The exercise, and possibly Mud's proximity, helped keep her mind off the accident and the images of the boy and his dog being knocked down, as Mud had promised. She shuddered and increased the speed on the treadmill. She needed to run harder.

———

THE BURN in Mud's body was nothing compared to the shredded agony of his heart. Griff. One minute laughing and goading him to race to their next stop, the next minute still. Lifeless. A crumpled mess buckled over jagged rocks. They said his neck had snapped on impact. That he'd felt no pain. Gone in an instant.

No. The pain was all Mud's. And the guilt. Why had he ever agreed to that trip? He'd thought riding bikes in the Canadian mountains would help his trauma from the terrible bushfire last year. Instead, it just brought more agony. Why had they ever started on the adrenaline cycle, thinking it was a good thing? Why were they ever inspired by Dad's stunt-man career? Even that had ended with a brain injury.

He shook his head and added another weight to the bench. Dad had always been larger than life. He sucked every moment out of every event. Put his hand up for the riskiest stunts. The biggest thrills. Of course, he trained hard for every feat but in the end it was still a gamble with life. And one day the wager didn't pay off.

But even left with a brain injury, Dad was still the happiest guy around, always laughing and joking, without a care in the world. Sure, he never performed another stunt and much of his fine motor skills were gone, but Griff and Mud had grown up thinking danger was a whole heap of fun. Death was something to be dared, toyed with, laughed at.

Two brushes with death in the past six months left Mud questioning all his beliefs. Was this life all there was? When you die, that's it? Or was there more afterward? And if there was, where was Griff now?

Mud grunted as he pressed the weights until the physical trainer told him to quit. The workout wasn't cutting it today. He sat up, giving his spotter a nod, and picked up a towel to mop his face. He glanced over at Amelia who ran hard on the treadmill. Was the exercise working for her? Her face was void of expression as she stared at the console, apart from a small crease between her brows. Despite that, he admired her effortless stride, all fluency of motion, toned, perfectly proportioned. Mud's mouth went dry as attraction struck him again.

With a huff, he turned his back and completed some cool down stretches. As if she would be interested in him, anyway. She was clearly mad at him about Bree. In his experience girls often stood together like that. She would carry her friend's offence and he would remain the bad guy, which was fair enough. He shrugged internally. In this case, he *was* the bad guy, and he had no way to remedy that.

Mud pushed the unfamiliar regret aside and strode over to Amelia. "How's it going?" he asked when her machine slowed and she unhooked her ear buds.

She nodded, breathless. "Good."

"I'm gonna hit the showers." He jerked a thumb toward the change rooms.

"Okay. I might as well finish up too."

Mud lifted his eyebrows. "See you out the front?"

"Sure." Amelia wiped her face which was barely flushed from the exertion.

Twenty minutes later she exited the gym dressed in flared jeans and a linen shirt, her long brown hair shimmering like silk in the sunshine. What he wouldn't give for a smile from those soft pink lips.

"So did it help?"

Amelia lifted one shoulder in a shrug. "A little, I guess."

Mud jingled her car keys. "Home?"

"I didn't know you wished for a career change."

Mud swerved his eyes to hers. "What?" Her face was straight, as though she hadn't said a thing.

"You want a job as my chauffeur now?" This time her lips twitched.

He chuckled, summoned his best British accent and bowed low with a flourish. "'Tis my pleasure to serve you, madam."

Amelia's hand flew to cover her mouth, but he knew she smiled by the way her eyes lit up and crinkled in the corners. A few seconds later, composed again, she headed to the car. "In that case, do you have any other ideas to keep my mind off yesterday?"

Mud fell in step with her, his mind going over different options. He wanted to keep himself busy as much as she did.

"Unless you have other plans, of course," she added.

"No," he said. She must have taken his silence as reluctance. "No plans. I'm just thinking." He unlocked the car and they both climbed in. "I often go clubbing. You know, dancing and all that." Would she go for it?

Amelia shook her head, lip clamped between her teeth. "I'd rather not."

"Yeah, well, they won't start till late anyway." Mud swallowed the twinge of disappointment that rose. He'd love to lose himself in music and probably some alcohol as well. But he might have to do that on his own. "How about horse riding? Have you ever done that?"

Her brows lifted. "Not for a long time. Probably since summer camp. There is a ranch about half an hour away if you want to go." She glanced at her watch. "Although it might be a bit late today."

Was that the real reason? Maybe Amelia didn't trust him enough to be around him for long. And he couldn't blame her. She probably thought he was some kind of skirt chaser, and that was a point on which he had no defense. He started the engine and reversed out.

"We could try kayaks on the lake." Amelia's voice broke into his thoughts. "That is, if you want."

"Sounds great. Let's do it." Mud headed out of the parking lot. Phew. At least she wasn't trying to avoid him.

This ten-minute drive seemed a little more relaxed than the previous one. Amelia jumped and reacted less than before. Hopefully that meant she was slowly getting over the shock, and she wouldn't need him anymore. Another pang of disappointment seared him. Mud was beginning to enjoy the company of this girl. He found Amelia's undemanding nature refreshing in contrast to his high-maintenance exes. She was comfortable. Not something he'd ever thought he'd appreciate. But right now it was a relief.

They pulled up at the rowing club and got out of the car.

"Are you sure about this?" Amelia asked. "I mean, you were pushing a lot of weights at the gym. Aren't your arms too tired to paddle?"

Mud narrowed his eyes. Was she trying to get out of it now? He offered her a smirk. "I'm a sucker for punishment." More than he'd let on. He needed more pain. Needed to feel as bad as he deserved. Or worse.

"'Cause you're not obliged to babysit me. I'm fine, really." She lifted her shoulders and chin as if to underline her words.

He released a harsh-sounding laugh. "No worries Meels.

We're just hanging out. Got it loud and clear. But do you want to row or not?"

Amelia stared at him for a moment. "Meels?"

"In Australia we shorten everything. Amelia. Meels. See?"

"So how did Mud come about?"

"That was an evolution," he explained. "Murchison. Murch. Murky. Mud. Make sense?"

"Sure. Right." Her face was unreadable, and she lowered her gaze. "Let's go."

Amelia introduced Mud to Hannah Gilbertson who set them up with a kayak, paddles and life vests and gave them the usual safety talk. Soon they were out on the water, a cool breeze blowing off the lake as they adjusted their strokes until they were in unison.

Kayaking on a calm lake was a far cry from whitewater rafting, but Mud still enjoyed it, laughing every time Amelia lost her rhythm.

"I haven't done this for a long time," Amelia admitted.

"You need to get out more," Mud told her.

Amelia sighed. "Yeah, probably. But I'm fine with reading and watching movies at home." Her back was to him so he couldn't see her face. She sounded wistful. Didn't she have anyone to take her out like this? No boyfriend on the scene? Surely, she spent time with Vi and the other girls regularly. Or was she that busy in the office?

"Well, I'm partial to a good movie, too." What else was he going to say? He didn't want to sound too compassionate and ruffle her independent feathers again. "And we've already established that I'm a softie for Disney fairy tales. Do you have any other favorites?"

"Mm-hmm." She nodded. "Superheroes."

Nice. She had good taste. "Batman or Superman?"

"Superman every time."

Even better. "I'm so with you on that."

"No way." He almost heard the roll of her eyes. "Like, *none* of my friends get it."

"Losers. All of them." He grinned at the back of her head.

"I enjoy other action-adventure too," Amelia added. "Oh, and natural disasters. I love natural disaster movies. *Twister*, for instance."

"Heck yeah. *Deep Impact. San Andreas. The Impossible.*" Mud almost laughed. They had similar taste in movies. "How about we catch a movie at the theater together one time?" *Oops.* Would that be too much? It wasn't like he was asking her out on a date or anything. Just friends with a common interest.

Sure enough, she went quiet. But a few moments later, she spoke up again as she slowly dragged the oar through the water. "I guess. There's a heritage theater in town that shows re-runs of old movies from time to time. It's run by an old school friend of mine. But I've never been."

Mud clicked his tongue. What a shame. How much had she missed out on? And why? "Well, we should remedy that. You can call me when something you want to see is showing. No pressure."

Amelia stayed quiet after that and he'd no clue of what she was thinking. When they returned the kayak, her face was once again deadpan, unreadable, although she thanked him for the enjoyable afternoon.

"Can you drop me at the car rental place? Are you up to driving yourself home?" Mud figured she'd had enough of him for the day.

Amelia drew a deep breath. "It's not far. I should be okay."

She looked anything but okay, her eyes wide and fearful.

"Look, you've got my number if you panic and need to pull over. I'm happy to come and help."

Her lips folded into a straight line as if she was determined. "I'll be fine."

Mud tried not to sigh audibly. Whatever. If she didn't want his help, so be it. He pulled up in front of the rental lot and moved to get out of her car when he remembered Sheriff Thompson's words.

"Hey, you still need to go to the police station and report on the incident."

Amelia stiffened. "I really don't want to think about it."

Mud tried to make his words gentle. "You realize the longer you leave it, the harder it will be for them to find the culprit?"

She groaned. "Okay, fine. I'll go first thing Monday."

"Do you need moral support? I'm happy to come along."

Amelia shook her head, biting down on her lip.

"Okay." Mud held back mild frustration. "I'll see you around, I guess." He got out of her car and headed for the rental office, not looking back to see if she even moved.

"Fine." Her voice caught him from behind. "Maybe."

Mud turned to see her standing next to her car and raised his eyebrow in question.

Amelia pinched her nose and adjusted her glasses. "I guess I could use some support."

CHAPTER FOUR

How it goaded her to be so needy. Amelia sat behind her steering wheel trying to summon the courage to drive the ten minutes home. Gripping the wheel tight, she started the engine, breathing deeply. She could do this. She could. It had never been a problem before. She just needed *not* to imagine people stepping onto the road ahead of her.

Loud music might help. Amelia turned the radio up so that it drowned out every noise, every thought, and pulled the car away from the curb. Okay, so this was working. Sure, her stomach still swirled with nerves, but she might make it home without caving. She concentrated on her breathing and the road rules and made it home without incident.

A rush of victory spread through her, and she laughed. Such a small thing and yet it felt huge. Though, as she let herself into her flat, she sighed. Sitting down with the sheriff would be another thing entirely. She was grateful for all Mud's support, but it still annoyed her to need help at all.

Ugh. Why did that concern have to come from someone she found so attractive? If she wasn't careful she would fall for him again. Why was he being so nice to her? And he even offered to take her to the movies. Like, was that meant to be an invitation for a date? Or was it pity that motivated him?

Her phone pinged. A message from Violet.

How are you?

Part of Amelia was grateful for friends who cared enough to check on her, but part of her hated answering the same questions over and over. She didn't really want to examine how she felt. She tapped out her usual response.

I'm fine.

Another ping.

Nick wants to know if Mud is behaving himself. And a laughing face emoji.

Amelia's lips twitched. What should she say? "No, he's up to all kinds of mischief?" But they would probably take her seriously.

He's being a perfect gentleman, believe it or not.

It's a miracle. LOL.

Yes, there truly is a God.

Amelia chewed on her lip hoping that wouldn't start Violet on a sermon about Jesus. Sure, Vi had changed a lot since attending that healing meeting last year—for the better —and Nick was a standout guy. But that didn't mean religion was for everyone, did it?

Sure is. Hey, do you think you'll be back in the office on Monday? No pressure.

Phew. No more God talk.

I have to make a statement at the police station, but after that will be fine.

OK. Great. I'll need you to go over the new Skydiving Europe tour guide. Make sure everything's covered.

Amelia smiled. This was an exciting step for Nick and Vi as a couple. They were setting up different skydiving tours around the world as a unique way of visiting those areas. They planned to take groups away in between their humanitarian efforts and wanted it all ready to go for soon after they were married. Well, after their honeymoon anyway.

No problem. I'll get onto it first thing.

Great. It's in your mailbox.

Amelia sent her a thumbs up emoji and put her phone down, only for it to ping again a few seconds later.

Are you sure you're OK?

Amelia released a long breath. Honesty time.

I won't deny it shook me up. But Mud really helped me get through it.

Well. Who would've thought?

I know. He surprised me.

I'm glad he was there for you.

Me too.

OK. Well, gotta go. And a love heart emoji.

Amelia groaned as she put her phone down. She hadn't even asked Vi how their trip was going. So selfish. Next time she would remember.

And speaking of remembering. She needed to pen some notes about what happened yesterday. Once in front of the sheriff she was certain her mind would go blank. Become emotional. Freeze again. Best to recall as much as possible right now and write it down. Even in the comfort of home it would be confronting. She closed her eyes for a moment then, with a breath of determination, gathered a glass of water and a notebook and sat back down on her sofa to face those memories.

Writing the vision that replayed in her mind brought tears to Amelia's eyes, blurring her words. Was she even keeping on the lines? She tugged at a tissue and blew her nose, drying her eyes before she continued. The car in front of her didn't stop. The boy and dog stepped into the road. The sickening thud. Amelia shuddered. What detail did she miss? Nothing came to mind. But at least she had the basics down. Probably Sheriff Thompson would ask for particulars of which she had no recollection.

As she closed the notebook, the notification on her phone sounded again.

So I guess you made it home alright?

Mud. She sighed. So thoughtful. Her heart did a little somersault. Well, it was more like a forward roly-poly, though she wished her heart wouldn't try any gymnastics at all. She didn't want to seem too enthusiastic so waited a few minutes before replying.

Yes, thanks.

Good to hear.

Amelia rose to make herself a mocha. She didn't want to encourage a conversation with Mud, assuming he would give up if she stopped sending messages back.

But it seemed he wouldn't let it go so easily. When she returned to the sofa, there was another text from him.

What you up to?

Preparing for my statement.

Good idea.

Not that she needed his approval, but it kind of made her happy. And before she thought twice, she asked him what he was doing.

Not much. Got the car. Now watching TV.

Anything good on?

Amelia waited a few minutes before a reply came through.

Wanna try something?

She screwed up her face. What did he mean? She sent him a couple of question marks.

I normally do this with Nick, but he's busy saving people or something.

Amelia snorted.

Poor Nick. What do you do?

So, we both stream the same thing, usually a reality show, and send commentary to each other for laughs.

Amelia's lips twitched. Sounded like fun.

OK. I'm in. How about Survivor?

Perfect.

They decided on an episode and hit play at the same time. Thus, the next hour flew by with a non-stop online chat where they tore apart contestants' attitudes, slammed some of their behavior, and tried to guess who the tribal council would vote off the island. Amelia ended up laughing harder than she had in a very long time. Who knew hanging out with someone via text message could be so fun?

It was almost like—like the year when her family sat together and laughed over *American Idol* auditions. There was no text messaging involved, though. That was the year Phillip Phillips won and released his song, *Home*.

Home. The thing Phillip Phillips made sound so welcoming, so safe, when in reality hers was falling apart. Because only a month later, Mom took off, unable to cope with Pa's deep depression. Amelia had just turned fourteen, trying for all the world to make her dad happy again, and also trying to find Mom and beg her to come back.

Amelia's pleasure of moments earlier slipped away like sandcastles under the waves. Even the popcorn she'd enjoyed ten minutes ago tasted like cardboard and she pushed it away. In its place came that familiar yearning she found difficult to articulate. She just wanted to be loved. Loved in a way that wasn't demanding and selfish.

Amelia shuddered. Yeah, right. That kind of love was only

in the movies or romance novels. She rose from the sofa, took her dishes to the kitchen and headed for her bedroom, suddenly bone tired.

Yet her phone still chimed every few seconds with notifications. Mud hadn't finished his side of the game. She typed a message that would shut him down for the evening.

Sorry Mud, I'm going to bed. Good night.

———

MUD STARED at the message again, re-reading it. What just happened? He and Amelia had been chatting happily but then she ghosted him for ten minutes followed by an abrupt *goodnight.*

Had he said something to offend her? He traced back through their conversation but couldn't see anything that stood out to him as inappropriate. What was her deal anyway? One minute she was so easy to get along with, the next she shut down. Completely.

Problem was, he really needed the company. The distraction. Nick was too busy in Africa. Manny, Nick's housemate, was glued to his computer at all hours, and apart from Bree, who didn't want to see him, he had very few acquaintances around Trinity Lakes. Without someone to talk to, hang out with, all his ghosts came out to play.

He didn't want to call Mum. Besides the time difference, they'd already shed so many tears together and he had zero desire to be ripped open again. Mum was nowhere near finished grieving. Plus, she was angry with him for staying in the US rather than going home to be with family. But he couldn't do it.

Mud wasn't able to face his happy-go-lucky father either. Because of Dad's brain injury, it was as though Griff's death was simply another thing to smile and nod about. As if the truth never passed the surface enough to touch his deeper emotions. A fact that made Mud sadder than ever. He didn't really want to grieve with Mum, but grieving with Dad could've been, well, cathartic.

There had to be something to do around this town until Nick returned. Mud recalled seeing an auto shop next to the rent-a-car place and an idea struck him. Perhaps he'd volunteer as a grease-monkey for a few hours here and there. He'd been a mechanic, after all, before his stint in the fire brigade. He had no working visa but he didn't care if he worked for nothing. At least he would be busy.

The following morning Mud drove back to where he'd seen the Trinity Lakes Auto sign and parked out front. As he approached the garage, a young man around the same age as him came out, wiping his hands on a rag before slinging it over his shoulder.

"Can I help you?" He thrust out a hand to shake.

"Not sure." Mud accepted the greeting. "I'm wondering if you guys need any help."

The man glanced toward the office. "I don't think we're hiring. Is that an Australian accent I hear?"

"Yeah, I'm Nick Gordon's mate. I'm not sure if you know him." You never knew in these smaller towns.

"Oh yeah. He's the one who's engaged to Violet Reynolds, right?" He nodded.

"That's the one," Mud confirmed.

"Yeah, I've seen him around. Seems like a great guy."

Mud tried not to roll his eyes. Every single person started with the "great guy" option when talking about Nick. "Yeah, anyway, I'm not looking for a job as such. Happy to volunteer." He laughed self-consciously. "I don't have the right visa to seek employment."

"But you're familiar with motors." It sounded more like a statement than a question, and a slight frown appeared between his brows. "Weren't you teaching skydiving last year?"

"I apprenticed as a mechanic. I did skydiving and worked as a tour guide on the side. More recently I started working with the fire brigade. So, I've serviced a few fire trucks when we're not fighting fires in Australia, but an engine's an engine, right?"

"OK. Well, I'll take you to see Bruce. He's the owner." He gestured for Mud to follow him to the office.

"Sure. What's your name again?" Mud asked as he fell into step with him.

"Brandon McAffrey. I'm one of the mechanics."

"Cool. I'm Mud." Mud almost had to take two steps for one of Brandon's strides. "Well, Mike Murchison, but everyone calls me Mud."

Brandon swung the door open and waved Mud inside. "Hey Bruce." He nodded toward an older man behind the counter who stopped typing on his computer when they entered. "This here is Mud from Australia. He's looking to volunteer with us for ..." He turned to Mud. "For how long?"

Mud shrugged. "Probs until the big wedding. Umm, mid-July."

Brandon swung back to Bruce. "Until July."

Bruce leaned his elbows on the counter and grinned. "Well, I'll be. I literally just got off the phone from a warehouse who wants us to service their entire fleet. I haven't given them an answer yet as I was going over the cost benefit figures to see if it was worth us putting on new a new mechanic to fulfill the job. You might be a godsend, son." He reached over to shake Mud's hand. "But, first things, first.

We'd better trial you and make sure you can do the work satisfactorily."

Still shaking his hand, Mud agreed. "I'm sure I can, and all the profit remains with you. I'd be happy to help."

Bruce turned to Brandon. "Get Betty ready."

Brandon nodded and headed into the workshop, leaving Bruce to introduce Mud to Ryder, their apprentice, then showed him around the workshop. When they emerged from the break room, Bruce pointed at a vintage Dodge Charger on a hoist. "See if you can get Betty-Blue running, son. That will be your test."

Mud glanced warily between Bruce and Brandon, who had reappeared. Was this some kind of prank? He was unable to read their expressions, so he shrugged. "Challenge accepted."

The others drifted off to continue their work leaving Mud to inspect the old classic. He started with all the normal checks—battery, spark plugs, oil, radiator, brakes, filters. When everything seemed in good order but the car still wouldn't start, he checked for other issues. With a chuckle, he shifted a fuse and moved to turn the key in the ignition. Betty-Blue came to life and purred like a kitten. Well, actually, roared like a lion when he revved the engine.

Clapping met his ears from behind. "Bravo." It was Bruce. "So you know what you're doing. And in good time too."

Mud turned to see him grinning. "I take it Betty-Blue is yours."

"1973 Charger. The love of my life." Bruce held his hand over his heart and had a twinkle in his eye.

Mud laughed. "Does that mean I'm hired without being, you know, hired?"

"Yeah, I think we could use you, son." Bruce nodded. "Can you start tomorrow?"

Mud rubbed the back of his neck, remembering his offer to Amelia. "Ah. I can. But I did promise to help someone first thing tomorrow. I'll come straight after that. Is that okay?"

Bruce lifted both hands in a gesture of surrender. "Hey, you're a volunteer. What am I gonna say? You get here when you can."

"Thanks, mate."

After saying his farewells Mud jogged to his car. Thank goodness for small mercies. That time messing around with Betty-Blue certainly kept his mind and body occupied and away from his dark thoughts.

And he remained relatively calm when he picked up Amelia the next morning. But he wondered if she would be more amicable today.

"How's it going, Meels?" He asked as she slid in beside him.

"Not looking forward to this is all I can say." Her face seemed remarkably calm despite the nerves she must be feeling.

Mud reached over and squeezed her hand. "You'll be fine. Deep breaths, remember?"

She pulled her fingers from his grasp but nodded. "Yes. Thanks."

In a side glance, her loveliness struck him again and he had an impulse to brush that silky hair away from her face so he could see her brown eyes clearly. *Woah, boy. We're not going there*. She was simply a friend he was helping. Nothing more. He cleared his throat. "Got myself a job."

Those brown eyes turned to him with a crease between them. "I didn't think—"

"Not a paid job." He pulled away from the curb, shifting his attention before he did something stupid to scare her away. "I'm volunteering at the auto shop."

A pause. "That's very generous of you."

Not really. Working was more self-serving than he would let on. "It's nothing."

"So the next time I see you, you'll probably smell like grease?"

Mud's heart skipped a beat. Did that mean she hoped to see him again? Did she … *like* the way he smelled? He made a note to himself to wear a good cologne the next time he hung out with her. Best downplay it, though. If he made a flirty response that would be it. "Yep. Grease, gas, rubber, sweat and goodness knows what else."

He glanced sideways to see her screw up her nose. Goodness, she had a cute nose. *Yikes. Stop it.* Mud puffed out his cheeks and focused on his driving.

"Could you add campfire smoke to that mixture? That would be an amazing combination."

Mud peeked at her again, but her face was dead-pan. What? So dry and goofy. He tried to keep his voice even and his face straight. "I mean, I love a campfire as much as the next bloke, but I don't think they have those in the garage. Might be considered dangerous."

She released a little sigh. "Disappointing."

A furtive look told Mud she gazed out the side window, so he was unable to read her face. He frowned. What was going on? Was she flirting with him? In a very weird and kind of hilarious way. Okay. He might as well keep playing along. "You have a thing for campfires, do you?"

"Yes. No." A gurgle of laughter escaped her. "Maybe."

Oh, but he'd like to hear that laugh again. It was like music. But for crying out loud, the sheriff's office appeared before the windscreen, thus ending this delightful conversation. Mud added to his list of mental notes—take Amelia for a campfire on the lake.

CHAPTER FIVE

The police station was a hive of activity. There were troopers coming and going and a queue of people waiting to see the officer on duty, some of whom looked like they'd lived a hard life. As they sat and waited to see the sheriff, Amelia wondered what their stories might be.

Mud startled her with a nudge and she turned to see him motioning with his chin toward a man in the line who wore a business suit. "What do you reckon? He's here to report vandalism to his Merc and his security cameras caught the culprit."

Amelia hid her smile behind her hand and whispered. "Or his wife's kicked him out and changed the locks and he wants advice on what he can do."

Mud's brows drew together. "Ouch. Such a happy thought. But, yeah, I s'pose." He scanned the queue. "And what about her?" He gestured toward a young woman with heavy eyes and fidgeting hands. "Drugs, you think?"

"Or she's here to fulfill her parole requirements, and she's antsy to get it over with, 'cause her kid is in the car with her deadbeat boyfriend."

"Wow, so judgy. Is your imagination working overtime or what?" Mud grinned at her.

"Too many movies and books." She rolled her eyes but couldn't hide her amusement.

Two troopers came in escorting a large man in handcuffs who sported a swollen lip and black eye. Mud immediately affected a slurred voice. "You've got the wrong man officer. The other bloke hit me first."

Amelia snorted. "A bar fight, do you think? Or he caught his wife cheating and beat the guy up."

Mud shifted sideways in his seat to look at her face on. "What's with the beef about relationships today?"

"What?" Amelia blinked rapidly, her mind scrambling.

"Every scenario you've come up with has been about husbands being kicked out, or losers or cheaters." His gaze intensified. "Did your parents ... you know ... were they difficult?"

She swallowed. How was he that insightful? Not that she wanted to regurgitate her past all over him, and especially not in a police station. "Well ... umm ... they—"

"Ms. Jones."

Relief washed through her as her name was called. Even if it meant jumping from a frying pan into an iron skillet. She glanced at Mud.

"Want me to come?"

She nodded, despite her mind yelling that she didn't need him. What was wrong with her?

Amelia sat with Sheriff Thompson for an hour, reliving the accident, going over every detail, retracing her steps after she got out of her car. But the one thing she was unable to help with was probably the most important—the driver and the car. The one who caused all the damage and fled the scene.

She took off her glasses and pinched her nose, then rubbed her brow. "I think it was a light-colored hatch back. Definitely a compact car. I think." Oh, why couldn't she be certain? It was as though the horror had wiped the memory of the moments following the impact from her mind.

"That lines up with other witness statements. Did you catch the license plate?" the sheriff asked for the third time.

"She's already told you, she didn't." Mud defended her. Sweet, but unnecessary. Amelia put a hand on his forearm to hint for him to be quiet.

"I'm sorry Sheriff. No matter how I try, I can't picture the car in front of me."

Sheriff Thompson didn't look happy. "Well, hopefully something will come back to you." He closed his notebook and leaned back in his chair.

Was this interview finally over? "Have you heard anything about the boy? Is he going to be okay?" She could really use some good news.

A smile appeared on the sheriff's face. A grim-looking smile, but it gave Amelia hope.

"Thankfully, he's going to be fine. His head hit the pavement and he has a moderate concussion, which they're observing, and he suffered heavy bruising and a fractured arm."

"He shouldn't have suffered any of it." Mud grumbled beside her.

"Amen to that." The sheriff rose from the table. "Now you call me if you remember anything else, Ms. Jones. No matter how insignificant you might think it is."

"I will, sir. You have my word." She didn't intend to be

unhelpful, but her brain refused to comply. She shook his hand and they left the station.

Amelia grunted as she walked. "I wish I remembered the car."

"It'll come back to you. Just relax." Mud's entire presence shouted "casual" as he strolled beside her, hands in his pockets. His button-down shirt was open, revealing a snug t-shirt beneath. A t-shirt which molded to his well-toned pecs.

Amelia shook herself. She shouldn't admire his muscles, no matter how ripped he was. She shifted her focus back to the conversation. "I might drive around town after work to see if anything triggers."

"That's a great idea," Mud agreed. "But wouldn't it be better if I drove you, so you can focus on looking and not driving?"

"Aren't you working at the auto shop today?" Surely he had better things to do than escort her everywhere.

"Yeah, but after that." He spread his arms wide. "My calendar is all open."

Amelia screwed her face up at him. "Who are you? The Mud I remember had a hot date at the club most evenings."

His eyes shuttered. "Not in the mood."

She eyed him for a moment. So, she wasn't the only one with ghosts in her past. Amelia wondered what had shifted him from being so carefree last year. Now and then she glimpsed something much heavier in his expression. What weighed on him so much? And why did he hide it?

"Or maybe," he said, his face clearing again, "driving around is my idea of a hot date." He turned to catch her gaze and her response with a sly grin.

Amelia stopped mid-stride and pretended to fumble in her purse for her keys, even though they had arrived in Mud's rental, because—mind blown. What did he mean by that? Surely, he was baiting her. Hadn't he said she wasn't his type? Her heart raced and heat flooded her cheeks. She needed to shut this down. "So, we're turning the air conditioner off. Is that what you're saying?"

He held up his keys, eyes twinkling, practically telling her he guessed what she was up to, then unlocked the doors. Amelia got in the car wishing they'd come in separate vehicles. Mud got in beside her but didn't start the engine—instead he faced her. "Look, I won't deny I'm enjoying hanging out with you."

Amelia bit down on her lip and averted her gaze. This was way too confronting. Him with his gorgeous eyes and smile, staring at her, waiting expectantly. A scenario she had dreamed about, hoped for last year, when she was invisible to him. And now he was here with her, telling her he liked her, or at least enjoyed being with her. Should she tell him she felt the same? But that would leave her open to heart break. She didn't need any of that. She opened her mouth to toss him a denial, but he spoke again.

"You have no reason to trust me, I get it." He swiveled back to face the windscreen. "I'm not asking for anything more than your company. But I'm saying I don't need an excuse to spend time with you. So, if you're free, I'm free. Simple as that."

A mixture of relief and disappointment flooded her. The friend zone. That's all this was about. Declaring he wanted to hang out like besties. Well, friendship was easy enough. And she wanted that more than she would ever admit. She pushed down the yearning for something deeper and nodded. "Got it. Friends."

———

No. No. No. Friends? That's not what he meant. Mud swallowed as he drove back to her flat. But, perhaps, in hindsight, that's what he should've meant. Because sure as anything he didn't need the complication of a relationship right now.

More and more, though, he was drawn to Amelia. For sure his interest had sparked, and that spark was catching into a flame. He knew well enough how fires behaved. Especially if there was plenty of fuel for them. Mud was in dangerous territory, an unfamiliar experience for him.

He'd lived with physical danger most of his life. Toyed with it. Dared it. Laughed in its face even. But emotional risk? That was entirely new and uncharted, and with Griff's death hovering in the background, this new emotion was overwhelming.

Before the tragedy with Griff, there had been the deadly bushfire in Australia that had taken several lives. Lives he should have been able to save. It didn't matter that others had told him there was nothing more he could've done. He still had to live with it. The dreams. The nightmares. Waking in a pool of sweat with the echo of screaming children still ringing in his ears.

What happened to those kids? Their life snuffed out before they'd barely experienced living. Was that all there was? Such a waste. He'd never believed in any kind of afterlife before that incident, but now he wanted to know. Was heaven real? Something deep within hoped those children lived on happily in some other place.

Mud snapped out of his reverie when they pulled up at Amelia's place and she moved to get out of the car. "Okay. See you tonight?"

"Sure." Amelia still seemed tight-lipped and her expression unsure, despite her answer.

"I'll pick you up at five thirty. That alright?"

"Yes. Fine."

Clipped words. Stiff posture. There was nothing in her body language that said she looked forward to seeing him again as she escaped into her unit. Had he misread her flirty banter? Not that it mattered. It appeared they'd agreed to be friends. For now, anyway. He breathed out as he drove to the auto shop. *Friends is good, Mud.* Friendship would be comfortable. Easy. No strings.

If only his heart would settle for that right now. It seemed to have a mind of its own. What a weird predicament to be in where his heart and his head were going in two different directions. Which should he listen to? Obviously, he should listen to his head. There was safety in logic. Wasn't there a saying that said "the heart is deceitful above all things"? So true. Where did that line come from, anyway? Some movie he'd watched? For the life of him, he couldn't remember.

None of this ruminating stopped him from thinking about Amelia all day. Her and Griff and the fire and Nick and Mum and Dad. Round and round it went. All while changing oil, cleaning spark plugs and testing brake pads. Loud music pumping through the garage's sound system did little to distract him. The only relief came from a few conversations with Brandon and Ryder.

It turned out Brandon was newly married and talked of nothing but his bride, Jodie, and Ryder loved to poke fun at the gushing groom. Their banter amused Mud and he laughed more than once.

"Hey." Brandon frowned at him although his eyes sparked with mirth. "You wait till you find someone. Of course, you won't find anyone as perfect as my Jodie."

Mud raised an eyebrow at him. "Who says I haven't already?" He tightened a nut, twisting the wrench hard.

Brandon gaped. "Have you?"

Mud chuckled. "Nah. Just messing with you." Amelia was more than attractive, but he was unsure if it would lead to anything else yet.

Brandon shook his head in wonder. "I tell you, though, when you find the right girl it's such a blessing. I can't even explain it. God has been so good to me."

"God, eh?" Another Jesus-lover. Mud couldn't escape them. He twisted the wrench again.

"Yes, God." Brandon put his tools down.

"Oho. You're in for it now," Ryder laughed. "He'll talk your ear off about Jesus more than he talks about Jodie."

Brandon shook his head with a good-natured laugh, but sure enough, he spent the next fifteen minutes telling Mud about how Jesus had changed his life. Apparently, he'd turned from being someone who ridiculed and judged others to someone who learned to speak with love and grace. He spoke of how he'd miraculously reconciled with a father he'd never known, and how he'd seen other's lives change in similar ways.

Mud had to admit it was pretty impressive, and it lined up with all the stories Nick had told him over the years. He'd never thought it necessary to entertain them as anything more than stories. But now? Now something in him wanted to learn more, but embarrassment prevented him from asking. Wouldn't he seem like an idiot? With so many years being Nick's friend, shouldn't he know it all already? Once again, he pushed his thoughts and questions back into the queue of other troubles that circled his mind.

When he left the garage, Mud stopped at the shops before heading to Nick's place. He picked up a decent cologne as per his mental note. When he finally washed, he made sure he scrubbed every bit of grease from his fingernails and double-checked there wasn't any on his face. Too bad if Amelia only wanted to be friends, he wanted to look and smell good for her.

On the dot of five-thirty he arrived at Amelia's and, surprisingly, she was already waiting for him out front. Hope lit within at her apparent eagerness, except when she got in the car, she seemed awkward. After securing her seatbelt she fidgeted with her purse.

"How was your day?" Mud pretended to ignore her agitation.

She blew out a breath. "Fine. I've been reading and checking a new tour guide brochure all day." She smiled, relaxing a little. "As much as I love words and books, if I never have to look at that document again, it will be too soon."

"A bit of screen fatigue, is it?"

"Understatement of the year." Her nod was emphatic. "Happy to look at something else for a change." She watched out the window for a moment as he headed towards town.

Mud surreptitiously checked out what she wore. Nice. Casual but flattering. Jeans and a floral blouse, with her long hair draping like satin around her shoulders. And he caught a waft of perfume—also floral. What would it be like to nuzzle into her neck and …?

"Do you get sick of looking at cars all day?"

Her voice interrupted his wandering imagination, which was probably a good thing.

"Because I'm now making you look at more."

Mud let out a gentle laugh. "Yeah. Nah."

Her face swerved toward him. "What does that mean?"

He chuckled again. "Sorry. It's an Aussie thing. Whichever comes last is the correct one."

Amelia stared at him briefly. "Right. So 'yeah, nah' is no, and 'nah, yeah' is yes."

"Correct."

"You're not sick of cars yet."

"Nope."

"Good. I mean, weird. But good."

Mud bit back another grin. "Any idea what we're looking for?"

Amelia huffed. "As much as I try, no. But I'm sure it was a small car and light in color."

"So, should we drive around town to see if any type of car triggers a memory?"

"That's the only idea I could come up with."

After driving up and down streets and walking through parking lots for an hour and a half, Amelia was more certain of the general make of the car. A silver hatch back. Problem was, there were so many of those around it would be difficult to pinpoint the responsible vehicle. And they weren't even sure if it belonged to a local.

"What if it was some random who happened to be passing through town?" Amelia's brow furrowed.

"That will make it difficult for anyone to find," Mud mumbled.

"I don't know what to do." She looked so helpless, biting on her lip like that.

"Let's take a break," Mud suggested. Continuing the search seemed pointless right now, and the cafes and restaurants on the main street called his name. "I'm pretty hungry. How about you?"

Amelia's gaze shifted from scanning cars to him, and the sudden contact with those hazel eyes made his heart skip a beat.

"I guess I could eat."

Yes. Mud did an internal fist pump while keeping it cool on the outside. "Any recommendations?"

She swiveled a hundred and eighty degrees, chewing on her lip. "We can try Giovanni's. I haven't been there since the opening last year." She shrugged. "Unless that's too much. We can go to Joe's Diner. Anything is fine."

"Giovanni's it is. Lead on, Macduff." He motioned her forward. If that was her first preference, that's what she'd get.

Amelia didn't move, but turned to him with a serious face. "If you're going to misquote Shakespeare, I don't think we can be friends."

Mud knew a moment of doubt. He had studied *MacBeth* in high school and it was something his dad had said heaps, but—

"It's lay on, Macduff," Amelia said with a roll of her eyes, "and it's about attacking, not following."

Mud studied her and soon figured she wasn't as grave as she made out. He kept his face as straight as hers as he leaned close. "Well then, I don't reckon you want me to be accurate in this case. Or are you looking for a fight?" How would she respond to that? He didn't wait to see but brushed past her and moved off toward the restaurant.

CHAPTER SIX

Amelia stared after Mud for a split second, then "hmphed" before hurrying to catch up to him. It was disconcerting, to say the least, having him so close and undoing her with his witty comebacks. But, goodness, he smelled so good. And looked good. Well, gorgeous actually. How was she supposed to keep him at arm's length? And why did her hands seem to have a mind of their own, yearning for the briefest contact with his? *Ugh.* She shoved her right hand into her jeans pocket and used her left to hang on to her purse.

Mud swung the door of Giovanni's open and stepped aside. "Benvenuti to youra dinner, signorina. Bellissimo." He kissed his fingertips.

He certainly was the charmer. Amelia tried to hide her smile by looking the other way as she passed. "Thank you, sir." She remembered her manners at the last moment.

If she thought walking next to him was unnerving, sitting across from him at a table for two was doubly so. It was much harder to avoid eye contact this way. Reading the menu and toying with her water glass only worked for so long.

"You never answered my question this morning." Mud turned serious after his first taste of gnocchi and bursting into *Bella Notte* from *Lady and the Tramp*.

How did he do that? Silly to serious in a heartbeat. "What question?" She was aware of what he meant but wanted to be cagey. "The one where you asked me left or right?"

"Funny." He rolled his eyes and shook his head. "Tell me about your family."

Amelia focused on her plate, twisting her fork through the delicious ribbons of fettuccine flavored with house-made pesto and grilled chicken. Did she want to open that can of worms? Part of her said "no," but another part of her wanted to share. She'd soon see how much of a friend he would be. Besides, she didn't need to go into too much detail.

"It was all good until I was about ten." She cleared her throat. "That was when my pa got hit with severe depression. Mum couldn't hack it and two years later, she split. Then Pa developed COPD, and I ended up caring for him until he passed away six years ago."

Mud released an expletive. "I'm sorry. I shouldn't have asked."

"It's okay. It's not like it's a secret or anything." She stabbed at a piece of chicken.

Mud still sat with his fork halfway to his mouth, eyes wide. "Can I ask? COPD?"

Amelia breathed out. "Chronic obstructive pulmonary disease," she said. "Emphysema might be more familiar."

Mud winced. "Nasty."

"Uh-huh." She took another mouthful of food, shaking off the grief those words created and tried to brighten her face.

"And what about *your* family? You haven't told me anything about them."

"Fair enough." He placed his fork down and folded his hands under his chin. "My dad was a stuntman."

"Was?" Now it was Amelia's turn to regret asking.

"Was, as in used to be," he clarified. "He smashed his head during a stunt about eleven years ago and now has an ABI—acquired brain injury."

Dismay gripped Amelia. She thought her story was bad. It must have shown on her face because he continued.

"It's all good. He lost some motor function and seems to have no emotion besides happy, but other than that, he's fine. Obviously, it put a stop to his career. Mum had to become the breadwinner, so worked all the time. And there's my brother Griff, and me. That's about it."

"You have a brother?"

"Y…yep. Yes." He nodded and returned to his food.

"I never had siblings. Vi's become the closest thing to a sister I have. I suppose so anyway. I guess I don't really know what I'm talking about." She should shut her mouth and stop blabbering. Or try a different angle. "Did you get up to lots of mischief as teenagers, or were you the kind of brothers who hated each other?"

"We sure did." Mud nodded, although his shoulders seemed to become rigid. "Mischief, that is." He coughed and wiped his mouth with his napkin. "You done?"

Amelia looked at her plate, which was only half empty, as was his. "I … I guess. I might get this to go, though." What just happened? Mud's face had completely clouded over.

He nodded, asked for the check, paid, then told her he'd meet her out front while she waited for her doggy bag and made a quick trip to the ladies' room.

Confusion followed her steps as they walked back to the

car. Mud had changed from the cheerful charmer to morose and quiet. When they got to his rental he stopped and looked at her. "Hey, I'm sorry." He rubbed his face. "I think I'm tired. Long day."

"You sure?"

"Sure."

And that was it. He drove her home in silence, then took off with nothing more than a "see ya."

———

BY THE TIME Mud got to the gym he barely held it together. Why had he answered any of Amelia's questions? He could've used diversion tactics like he normally did. Instead, he had opened up a tiny crack, and yet it felt like a dam bursting. He needed to punch something. Hard.

He aimed straight for the boxing bags and let loose—the only way he knew how to tame the roaring maniac inside him. It wasn't as though he pictured anyone's face as he rained down punches on the bag. It was more so a release for the grief that churned. And if it hurt while he did it, so much the better.

If only he could call Griff. His brother would've listened and vented with him. But that was one call he'd never make again. A couple of weeks ago he'd forgotten for a second, dialed him and heard Griff's voicemail message. It tore him apart anew. His brother's laughing face always flashed before him, an instant before the image of his brother flying over the handles of his mountain bike and the deathly crack that followed.

Once Mud had spent his energy on the boxing bag, he pushed himself for another half an hour at speed on the treadmill. Exhaustion finally caught up and he headed home.

Several beers before he turned in ensured a deep sleep, so those ghosts would finally leave him alone for a few hours. Unless the nightmares came.

———

AMELIA LAY WIDE AWAKE. Not replaying her conversation with Mud, strangely enough. Not dwelling on her family issues. Instead, her mind traveled to her ex, Cody. Perhaps the way Mud suddenly cooled toward her had something to do with remembering Cody, but she couldn't fathom why.

Cody had been great to start with. Handsome, tall, romantic. Just like a Hallmark movie come true. He said all the right things and did all the right things, and she fell for him hard. As things progressed they discussed moving in together, a prospect she didn't exactly oppose, but that's when she started having second thoughts.

It began with simple expectations that irked her. He asked her to pick up his dry cleaning, to bring him lunch at work, to dash to the supermarket for him. Soon it developed into incidents like inviting her on a date for a picnic, then asking her to organize and bring the food. To top it off, he told her about decisions he needed to make, asked her for advice, or more often, asked her to decide for him.

In the end, she felt like a caddy, a servant, a care giver, and even a mom, rather than a valued partner. She had spent six years caring for her father's every need. She didn't want to go back there again. When Cody begged her to stay with him, told her how much he needed her, that was the last straw. The thought of being trapped with that level of demand again almost made her physically ill. No, thank you.

Amelia ended things with him and had cried off men ever since. Until she met Mud. But now she feared he had his own sense of lack, and she didn't want to face that possibility. There was no way she would let him get close while that doubt hung over her head, no matter how charming and friendly he might be. She couldn't face that possibility.

Over the next few days she found her fears confirmed as he seemed to have ghosted her. Not that she tried to contact him, either. She didn't need that complication, thank you very much.

But on Thursday afternoon suddenly a message came through.

Hey Meels. I think I found the car.

GREAT FRIEND HE WAS. Mud's behavior the other night embarrassed him, and he hadn't contacted Amelia since. Sure, he'd picked up his phone several times a day to message or call her, but words failed him. After telling her he was there for her and wanted to be around her, he'd completely let her down.

Thankfully, work at the auto shop kept him busy and pulled him somewhat out of his doldrums. Better than sitting around with nothing to do but watch TV, anyway. And he was getting along with the guys in the garage pretty well, which led to his sudden message to Amelia.

She would probably hate the randomness of his text with no preamble "hello", "how are you," or "I'm sorry." He'd have to make up for a lot later. The thing was, during one of his conversations with the guys, Brandon mentioned how Jodie had damaged his car not long before they were married.

"She borrowed it to take the girls to Spokane on a shopping trip for bridesmaid's dresses. They barely made it out of town before a fawn ran out in front of her."

"Dude. No." Mud winced. "Were they okay?"

Brandon nodded. "Thank God, only the fawn sustained any injury, but the front of my truck was pretty messed up."

"Far out." Mud's brain started working in overdrive. "We never thought about that."

"What are you talking about?" Brandon frowned.

"The hit and run that Amelia witnessed. A dog died, and a teenager ended up in hospital. Surely there must have been damage to the car."

Brandon's eyes widened. "Absolutely. For sure."

Mud pulled out his phone. "I'm gonna call the sheriff." He checked his wallet for the business card he'd taken from Sheriff Thompson and dialed. Brandon stood there watching and listening, his brow creased.

"Hi, Sheriff Thompson. It's Mud. Amelia Jones's friend."

"How can I help, Mud?"

Mud put the phone on loud speaker. "Have you guys looked into damaged vehicles?" He didn't want to sound like he was telling the sheriff how to do his job, but he was curious as to their processes.

"We've considered it, of course, but without a definite make or model, it's a little difficult, added to the fact we're pretty swamped here already. We've sent officers around to some of the local auto body repairers, but haven't learned anything useful yet."

Mud glanced at Brandon who shook his head and jerked his thumb over his shoulder, mouthing words Mud couldn't read.

"Right. Thanks Sheriff. Umm, Amelia thinks it's a silver hatchback. Do you mind if I keep a lookout? I'll contact you if I find anything."

"A silver hatch. Noted. Thanks, Mud. I appreciate all the help I can get, but please don't confront the driver if you find them." The sheriff rang off and Mud looked at Brandon again.

"What were you trying to tell me?"

"I'm not sure, but I don't think the cops have been to the body shop next door. I haven't seen any patrol cars around, anyway. We can go check if you like." Brandon grabbed a rag and started wiping his hands down.

"Yeah, well, it sounds like they're flat out investigating several cases at the moment." Mud followed suit.

Brandon huffed. "It's true. I know a guy who was brought in to help with a case about a little kid called Charlie. They found him abandoned in the park, but no one has any information about him."

"Dude. Who does that kind of thing?" Mud shook his head, aghast.

"I know, right?"

"Well, let's see if we can give them a hand."

They strode toward the crash repairer. Brandon was familiar with the staff. They'd repaired his own truck recently. It seemed they often referred business between the two garages. A casual conversation revealed that a silver hatchback with front-end damage had been brought in. The owner had previously removed the bumper and grill intending to DIY his repairs, but there was damage to the radiator, so he'd ended up bringing it in. Circumstances that sounded dodgy to Mud, like the owner was trying to cover up something.

"Can we see it?" Brandon asked.

"Sorry, man," Steve, the business owner, replied. "It went home yesterday."

Disappointment coursed through Mud, but he wasn't about to let go. "Are you able to give us information about the owner?"

Steve pressed his lips together and looked from one to the other of them, as if he was trying to decide. He opened his mouth to answer, but Mud jumped in.

"Look, this bloke possibly ran a kid and his dog down and then took off. We need to find him."

Steve's eyes narrowed and he uttered an oath. "What do you need?"

"Rego, name, address. Whatever you've got."

"Rego?" Steve's brows furrowed.

"Um, license plate I guess." Mud shrugged, suspecting the terminology might be different in America than he was used to.

"Hey, aren't there privacy laws to consider?" Brandon looked uncomfortable.

Mud gritted his teeth but tried to remain pleasant. "The police are going to come around and ask for it, eventually. What does it matter?"

Steve seemed to agree with him. "Forget privacy. If this guy didn't care enough to stop and own his mistake, he doesn't deserve protection."

Brandon lifted his arms in an expression of surrender. "Okay. Okay. Just sayin'. Your call, Steve."

Steve turned to Mud. "Give me five." He jogged off to his office.

"You won't do something stupid, will you?" Brandon asked Mud when they were alone.

"Stupid?"

"Like, go around there and beat up on the guy or something."

Mud scoffed and put on his best Rocky Balboa accent. "Nah. I'll get Amelia to beat him up instead."

Brandon's eyes widened and his mouth gaped ready to make some kind of exclamation.

"Relax dude," Mud laughed. "Jokes. But I will take Amelia around to see if she recognizes the car. If she does, we hand the info over to the cops. Happy?"

Brandon seemed relieved. "Happier, I guess. Just don't take the law into your own hands, okay?"

With a few reassurances to Brandon, and the car details in hand, Mud sent a text to Amelia. Truth be told, if this was the guy responsible for the hit-and-run, Mud wouldn't mind teaching him a lesson. Or two. But like Brandon said, he should leave that to the police.

His phone vibrated as a new message landed in his phone. *Where is it?*

Right. No small talk from her either. What did he expect? His gut clenched. What an idiot he'd been. There was nothing he'd like more right now than an easy conversation with Amelia. A fun conversation. But now he'd have to wade through apologies and explanations before he got back to that. *If* he could get back to that. Had he done his dash with her?

He gripped the phone between his knees and tipped his head back, eyes closed. Regret was a new thing for him. One he wished he didn't have to experience. But emotions seemed to be all he had at the moment. One feeling after another. Sentiments he barely contained and even less he processed. He groaned.

And then his phone rang.

Amelia.

His heart flipped and flopped and he almost dropped his phone, but pressed the answer button before it was too late. "Hey." Goodness, he sounded breathless in his own ears.

Silence for a heartbeat. Two. "Hey."

What to say? What to say? Mud reckoned she probably

wanted to hear about the car more than anything else, so figured to start there. "I have an address—"

But she'd spoken at the same time. "What have you got?"

They both laughed awkwardly. Far out. He was going to have to clear the air first. "Amelia, I'm so sorry for the way I acted the other day. And for giving you the silent treatment for days on end. I'm—I'm not myself lately."

More silence, except for her breathing at a rate that seemed quicker than normal. "Are you going to tell me what happened?"

"With the car?"

"With you."

Mud almost heard the eye roll. But he couldn't tell her about Griff. It was too hard. What else should he say, though? Skim the surface, perhaps. "My family ... well, it's complicated. I find it hard to talk about them." He paused and swallowed. "I'm sorry I shut down on you." That would have to do. For now, anyway. He didn't really want to have a deep conversation on the phone.

"Hey, I understand." Amelia's voice flattened. "I'm not a fan of airing out my problems either, but I mean, if we're supposed to be friends ..."

Mud sucked in a deep breath. Time to man up. "Yeah, I should have been more open with you. It was cruel and uncalled-for. Especially after telling you I enjoy your company."

"It was definitely a shock."

"Do you think you can forgive me?"

Another couple of heartbeats passed. "I guess."

Mud realized he held his breath. Since when did a woman's absolution mean so much?

"*Raiders of the Lost Ark* is showing at the heritage cinema next weekend." Amelia's voice held a note of amusement. "If you can sit through that with me, I'll consider it restitution."

"No problems at all, Meels." Mud's heart swelled, though he kept his voice dry. "You tell me when."

"Okay. But first things first. What have you learned about the car?"

"I have an address. This car had some front damage and fits your description. Wanna go check it out? See if you remember it?" He remembered this friendship might still be fragile. "I mean, you can go by yourself if you want ..."

"No. That's fine. Pick me up in an hour."

CHAPTER SEVEN

Amelia probably should have stayed mad at Mud. Should have made him plead more, pay more. But she couldn't do it to him. Besides, this crazy yearning for the friendship he offered refused to be silenced. In three short days she realized how much she missed his company already.

She tried to hide her smile as she sat beside him in the car. Really, she should focus on this suspicious vehicle, but Mud's presence sent her thoughts and emotions tumbling. How did he look even more gorgeous than a few days ago? Those dark, collar length curls that practically begged her fingers to entangle themselves. Broad hands that would easily encompass hers. Amelia's heart fluttered and she turned her gaze out the side window. These weren't thoughts of friendship.

Mud concentrated on the GPS guidance so hopefully didn't notice her blush. What a stroke of luck it was a local. Mud impressed her even further with his clever investigation into the idea of a damaged car. Amelia chewed on her lip. It meant a lot that he'd thought of her enough to find the car.

"Here we are." Mud drew her from her reverie. "Now, the car's already repaired so you won't see anything wrong with it, but see if it triggers any memories."

"Where am I looking?" Amelia twisted in her seat to look all around.

Mud pointed to a house across the street. "Over there. The one in the driveway."

Amelia scrambled out of the car and ambled toward the hatchback Mud pointed out, her stomach sinking. "Oh." She shivered as memories assailed her.

"What's happening?" Mud came up beside her.

"That's it. That's the car." Her whole body trembled.

Mud immediately put a firm arm around her shoulders and held her tight. "It's okay," he whispered in her ear, his voice both soothing and electrifying. "Are you sure?" With his free hand he clasped hers, the pressure bringing even more calm.

"YODELL." She read the personalized license plate with Washington above it. "As soon as I saw it, it all came back to me." All the moments she hadn't been able to remember before were back. How that car had driven through the pedestrian red light, the images of the boy going under the wheels, and YODELL disappearing down the street without a pause. A guttural sob burst from her and she buried her face into Mud's shoulder.

His arms surrounded her fully and she allowed his strength to steady her for a moment.

"It's okay. You did great," he murmured into her hair.

Amelia pulled her ragged thoughts together and leaned back from Mud, and although his arms loosened, he didn't let go. His eyes, wide, so full of compassion, were grazing every inch of her face. If she didn't know any better she'd think he was about to—

She pushed away from him, breaking the moment. "I need to go to the police."

Mud released her and cleared his throat. "Sure." He stepped back towards his hire-car. "Do you want to go now or in the morning?"

Amelia glanced at her watch. The afternoon was gone and it was more like dinner time. Her stomach gurgled as if to establish that fact, despite the dismay that had settled on her nerves with the return of her memories. She wasn't ready to be parted from Mud yet but was hesitant to suggest they eat together again after the other night. "The morning's fine."

Once inside the car, she chewed on her lip before asking, "Are you busy tomorrow?"

Mud shrugged and started the car. "I mean, other than the auto-shop, I have nothing pressing."

"Because Nick and Vi are flying in tomorrow and I'm driving to Walla Walla to collect them."

"I thought they were gone for a couple of weeks." His brow furrowed.

Amelia smothered a smile with her hand. "They *have* been gone a couple of weeks. They were already away for a while before you arrived. Didn't Nick tell you?"

Mud shrugged again as he drove. "Probably. Come to think of it, he did. I'm not always great at taking in details."

"You'd better not stand me up at the theater on Saturday."

"I would never." Mud feigned offence.

At least, she figured it was pretend by the way his hand covered his heart and he over dramatized the words. Amelia hid another smile.

"Anyway, are you inviting me to come to the airport?"

Amelia kept her gaze on the passing traffic. "Maybe."

"Well, considering Nick is my best mate, I probably should show my face."

"That's what I thought." Partly. Amelia figured he'd like to see his friend, but she mostly hoped for more time with Mud.

Mud's car slowed and he parked outside her unit. "What time tomorrow?"

Amelia drew in a deep breath. She must use restraint, although she really wanted to ask him to come inside. "I'll see Sheriff Thompson first thing, then I need to do some work in the office. I can pick you up after lunch. Their flight doesn't arrive till late afternoon."

Mud seemed equally conflicted. He rubbed his hands up and down his thighs. "Sure. I'll bring snacks for the trip."

Amelia's lips twitched. "It's less than an hour away."

"So?" He shrugged. "Snacks are good."

"Okay. If you say so." Amelia didn't mind a good snack herself. She wondered what kind he would bring. Oh, but she needed to get out of his car before she did or said something stupid. "Well, see you tomorrow then."

Mud's chin jerked down. "Yeah. See ya."

As she walked up the path to her front door, he called out to her.

"Hey, Meels."

She turned to see he'd rolled down his window. "Yeah?"

"Thanks for being so ... understanding. And gracious. You know."

Amelia offered him a genuine smile. "You're welcome." She turned and hurried inside before temptation drew her back to him. Because as much as she hadn't wanted it, Mud was getting under her skin. And possibly into her blood and bones as well. She leaned against the closed door and sighed.

What was she going to do about him? She shook off her longings and tried to put him out of her mind. Tomorrow was another day, and she'd deal with him then.

But before that, she had to go to the police station. She headed there straight after breakfast the next morning. Once again, there was a wait because of the constant stream of people wanting their complaints heard or issues looked into. Amelia smiled as she recalled guessing people's stories with Mud. But had she been so transparent that he'd guessed her troubled upbringing? She'd never thought her heartache leaked out so obviously. Had Violet seen it too?

She remembered something Vi said when they were in France: "Jesus loves you. He's loved you since before you were born and will love you forever, regardless of whether you return that love."

Amelia pondered the words now. Did she really appear so lacking in love that Vi *had* to say something? Amelia never wanted to come across as desperate, but had she? Inadvertently? She closed her eyes. It was true, though. The yearning to be wanted, desired, loved chased her every step. Even more so in the last year or two. Vi told her the answer was in Jesus. Amelia shook her head. No, she wasn't so needy she had to find religion.

A door opened and the sheriff popped his head out. "Ms. Jones? Come through."

Amelia followed him to a small interview room.

"Sorry about the wait. This year has been crazy."

"It's fine." Amelia sat in the chair he indicated.

"What have you got for me?"

She handed him a piece of paper with the details of the silver Ford hatchback on it. "We found the car."

Sheriff Thompson read the note. "You're certain?"

Amelia nodded emphatically. "As soon as I saw the YODELL plate, it all came back to me."

"You recognized the license plate?"

"Yes. Correct. That's the car."

"Okay. Great." The sheriff blew out his cheeks. "We'll look into it. It's a relief to have a solid lead on this, I have to say."

"I'm relieved too, sir. You can't imagine how awful I felt when I couldn't remember anything." She stood up. "Any news about the poor boy?"

"I understand he's going home today or tomorrow. His arm will be in a cast for a while, but other than that he's recovering nicely." Sheriff Thompson pushed the chairs back under the table and motioned her towards the door.

"That's good to hear."

"Another relief, I'm sure," he agreed. "Now, we may need to contact you again once we find this driver. Is that okay?"

"Of course." As if she would say no. Hopefully, they would apprehend the guy soon, ending this entire episode.

MUD FINISHED TOPPING off the oil in the Mustang he was servicing, singing *Mustang Sally* as he worked. He'd spent a lot of time in cars with Amelia in the last week, and today would be no different. He grinned at the lyrics that played. Unlike the song, he was in no hurry for Amelia to stop. He closed the hood and wiped his hands, shifting gear to a different tune. *On the Road Again.*

"Man, you haven't stopped singing all morning." Brandon slapped him on the shoulder. "You got a girl or something?"

Mud shrugged but found it hard to hide his smile. "Off to pick up Nick, this arvo—afternoon. My best mate." That was a clever diversion if ever he knew one.

"Cool. That'll be great."

"Yeah, it will." More than great, if it was as fun as he expected. "Well, I'm done for today. See ya tomorrow." He tossed the rag and backed away from Brandon.

"Enjoy your afternoon, Mud." Brandon saluted him.

Mud practically skipped to his little rental and hurried home to clean up. She'd be there in half an hour. Just enough time to throw down a sandwich and take a shower. As the water ran over his head and shoulders, he remembered last night and how he'd been so close to kissing her. It was like she belonged in his arms. She fit so perfectly, so snuggly. His disappointment at her breaking away warred with guilt, because he shouldn't be heading in that direction at all. He was a mess, as though pieces of his soul leaked out like water, and he'd tried to stop up the holes with mesh wire. Nothing worked.

After saying goodbye to her last night, he'd gone straight to the gym and pushed weights until every muscle screamed at him. Then he'd headed home and consumed hours gaming with Manny. Although, granted, Manny turned in at eleven leaving Mud to compete with online gamers until the early hours. Car racing. Shoot-'em-up. Anything that kept his adrenaline pumping and his mind away from Griff and that deadly inferno.

Yeah, he should really stay away from Amelia. He wasn't good news by any stretch of the imagination. But the motivation to keep his distance ranked at minus fifty-two thousand, while the draw to be near her sat around eleven million. There was no way to fight it.

A car horn sounded as he splashed cologne on his jawline. Mud jogged to the kitchen, grabbed an energy drink from the fridge and the bag of snacks he'd purchased, and headed out the door.

Strange. That wasn't Amelia's green Mini. It was a black Lincoln Navigator. His steps slowed as he approached and the passenger window lowered. Amelia.

"I thought we'd all be more comfortable in the Reynolds' SUV. There are six of us, after all. And Tony's driving."

Mud climbed in the back seat as disappointment settled in his stomach. She wasn't even going to be next to him for the ride? "Hey, Tony." Mud remembered Violet's security guy from last year. "You didn't travel overseas with them this time?"

Tony's lips curved up. "Nick's pretty good at looking after Violet. I've become redundant to that extent. Besides, Mr. Reynolds went with them on this occasion. I'm glad I can be useful today."

Amelia twisted in the front seat, her eyes bright. "What yummy treats did you bring?"

Mud pretended to look hurt. "Is that all you care about? You're using me for food now?"

"Good snacks are the way to a woman's heart, didn't you know?" Her lips twitched.

Too bad if there was another listening ear, Mud wasn't about to let that flirty look slide. "Promise?" He wiggled his eyebrows. "'Cause I have some pretty good stuff here."

She shifted her body back, looking out the front window, but he still saw the color that infused her cheeks and grinned.

He noticed Tony watching him in the rearview mirror then speak to Amelia. "Isn't it a bit rude to sit in the front with me and still take advantage of all his food?" Tony winked at him as he stopped the car. He turned to Amelia. "Go on, get in the back and keep your friend company."

Amelia seemed to pause for a moment before doing as

AMANDA DEED

she was told. Mud mouthed a thank you to Tony, who
nodded as he continued driving.

"So, do you wanna see what I have?" Mud held the bag to
his chest.

Amelia crossed her arms. "This was a bad idea. I never
thought you'd turn against me, Tony." But her lips still
tweaked up in the corners.

"Who says I've turned against you?" Tony teased. "I'm
saving you from the sore neck you would get from craning
your neck all the way to Walla Walla."

"Yeah. Whatever." Amelia rolled her eyes good-naturedly,
then with a sigh she turned to Mud. "Okay. Show me."

Mud dumped the contents on the seat between them.
Peanut butter cups, Cheetos and Oreos spilled out, among
other chips and candy.

"Oh, my favorites." Amelia clapped. "How did you guess?"

He didn't, but hey, if it worked in his favor. "I'm an excellent judge of character." He laughed. "But really, these Oreos
have nothing on our Tim Tams. Just saying."

"No way." Amelia shook her head.

"Have you ever tried a Tim Tam?"

"No."

"Well, you cannot make that claim."

"Pfft." Amelia waved him away as she shoved a cookie in
her mouth.

Mud leaned back in his seat and sipped at his energy
drink. My, but he liked her when she was relaxed like this.
Not trying to hide her laughter and playing along with every
ridiculous remark he made.

The time flew by as they traveled and before they knew it,
they'd arrived at the airport.

"Okay. You kids jump out and find them. I'll circle back
here and pick you up in twenty minutes," Tony instructed.

"Sounds like a plan." Amelia waved goodbye to the driver as they headed inside the terminal.

Minutes later, arms flew in all directions as they exchanged hugs and welcomes with the home-comers.

"So good to see you, bro." Nick thumped Mud on the back repeatedly.

"You too dude." Mud's heart settled in that moment. Just a little. His best mate was here. Someone he could lean on, and that gave him relief he couldn't explain.

"How was the trip?" Amelia asked Violet after they'd embraced like long-lost family.

"Fantastic," Vi answered. "Oh my goodness, but you should have seen how cute the orphans were."

Nick lifted his eyes to the ceiling. "She's gone clucky, mate." He pulled a face at Mud.

Mud laughed. "And you love it. Don't even try to deny it."

Nick gazed at his fiancée and his expression softened. "Guilty as charged." He dropped a kiss on the top of her head and Vi looked up at him with such tenderness it made Mud's heart swell.

How good would it be to have a relationship like that? Mud chanced a glance at Amelia who seemed busy checking out her shoes. If only she would look at him like that. *What? No.* Wasn't he trying to avoid that very thing? Even though every day that he saw her, he realized more how amazing she was. He smothered a cough, trying to dislodge these stupid emotions. A permanent attachment wasn't something he desired.

He simply needed to get over Griff and everything and get back to normal. And the only way to do that was to talk to Nick. Like, properly talk. Man to man. Heart to heart. And the sooner the better.

Late that night, when they'd finally parted from the girls

and got back to Nick's place, they sat together in the lounge room with sodas, cheese and crackers.

"You haven't told me, bro, what made Griff pull out of your trip?" Nick eyed him. "You two didn't have a blue, did you?"

Mud coughed, suddenly choking on his cracker. There must be razor blades stuck in it, the way it caught in his throat. "Nah, not that." If only it were that. He got up, at once antsy, and paced around the room. This was his chance to get it out. To talk about his feelings. But they were so big, like an explosion about to go off. The fuse was lit and it was only a matter of time.

"What then? Tell me about it." Nick leaned his head back against the cushions, obviously getting comfortable for the story ahead.

Mud wiped his hands down his jeans. "Okay. Well, we were having a great time at first. We were mountain biking on Whistler. You knew that, yeah?"

"Yeah. I bet those trails were sick, right?"

Mud laughed though it sounded weak in his ears. He continued walking around the room, staring at the walls, the roof, the furniture. "Yeah. They were sick alright. Griff wanted to go on the higher difficulty trails. Which is fine. He's completely capable of riding those paths. But then ... then ... he hit an exposed root. The bike flipped and Griff ... well ... he landed on a rock. Head first. And he ..." Mud finally looked at Nick whose eyes were closed. Asleep. Mud's shoulders sank, their weight dragging him to the floor, silent sobs shaking him. "He died, Nick. Griff died."

CHAPTER EIGHT

Amelia entered Violet's home on Friday to the smell of freshly brewed coffee. Oh, it was good to have her friend home again, even if it meant she'd have to listen to the never-ending wedding plans and Vi gushing over Nick.

"Morning," she called out as she wiped her shoes and folded her umbrella into the stand.

"Whew, crazy weather out there." A sudden rainstorm had let loose on her way to work and despite the umbrella, Amelia needed to mop down her arms.

Vi's head popped around the corner. "Good morning."

Her smile was bright, although ... "You look tired."

"Yes. A bit of jet lag, you know." She shrugged, then bit her lip. "Apparently Nick fell asleep on Mud last night."

"Poor Mud." Amelia rolled her eyes. "They were probably having one of their inane conversations, anyway."

"Well, he was gone before Nick had a chance to apologize this morning, so I hope it's all okay."

"I'm sure they'll be fine. Mud would understand." Amelia

finished wiping herself down and stepped into the kitchen. "That coffee smells amazing."

"Want some?"

"Of course."

With hot coffees in hand they moved to the office and sat in the lounge chairs. Violet wanted to catch up on the past couple of weeks before they got to work. Violet told her all about their trip to Africa, showing photos of the orphans she'd mentioned and the work that was going on over there. After that, Amelia updated her friend slash boss on everything she'd worked on while they were away.

"And in the middle of all that, the hit-and-run happened," she said as she finished.

"That must have been awful. Were you okay?" Vi's eyes widened with concern.

"I was fine, apart from some shock. I still shudder every time I remember it, but it's been good to focus on helping the police rather than the experience." Amelia sipped her coffee.

Violet reached out a hand and put it on her knee. "I'm sorry you only had Mud to lean on."

Amelia swallowed her coffee while shaking her head. "Actually, he was great. I wonder if it's because he's a fire-fighter. He knew exactly what I needed."

Vi sat back again, her eyes lit with surprise. "Really? Well, the Lord works in mysterious ways."

"The Lord?" Amelia didn't comprehend her meaning.

"We weren't here to help you so we did the only thing we could—we prayed. But Jesus knew exactly what you needed and he sent Mud, knowing he would be the perfect help." Violet's face glowed. "And also, I would never have sent Mud to you if we had other options. Never realized he had that capacity. See, God knows what he's doing." She ended with a laugh.

Amelia sat staring at her friend, trying to digest the words. Surely it was all a big co-incidence. "Why would God be interested in helping me?"

Vi laughed again. "That's easy." She scooted closer and gave Amelia a hug around the shoulders. "Because he loves you."

Amelia sipped her coffee. There it was again. Those words she'd remembered the other day. Was it possible? Had God brought Mud along at the right time to help her when she needed it most? Memories of her father flashed through her mind. If that was the case, why didn't God show up when she'd had to care for Pa on her own all those years?

"Do I seem needy to you?" Amelia's voice seemed hoarse in her own ears as she forced the words out.

A sound of protest escaped Vi's mouth, but she squeezed Amelia's shoulders again. "Never. You must be the most independent person I've ever met. But that doesn't stop the Lord from loving you or wanting a relationship with you." She shifted back to her original position on the sofa. "And it's okay to lean on Him. You don't have to carry everything by yourself. He's got massive shoulders. You should try it sometime."

With those words, Vi picked up her mug and shifted to her desk ready to start work, leaving Amelia pondering. She tightened and loosened her grip on her coffee cup. Once upon a time she'd leaned on Mom, but she left. She'd tried to lean on Pa, but he got sick and drained every ounce of her energy. What if she leaned on God and became dependent only to find herself deserted again? Violet said He was rock-solid reliable. But how could she be sure? Wasn't it better to depend on herself?

Amelia put all these thoughts out of her head as she worked, focusing on another new tourism guide Violet was creating. This involved lots of brainstorming, vision board-ing, and analysis, which kept her mind busy and away from the troubling ideas Violet had planted in her head.

It was late in the afternoon when she received a call from Sheriff Thompson.

"Hello, Sheriff." She injected enthusiasm into her tone as she answered the phone. "Do you have good news?"

"Unfortunately, no." His voice was tight. "The owner of that vehicle has a solid alibi. He was running a tutorial at the time of the incident."

"How is that possible?" Amelia's stomach tensed. "I saw the car. Was it stolen?"

Sheriff Thompson released an impatient sniff. "He still has the vehicle in his driveway, so no."

Amelia felt as surge of embarrassment. *Stupid.* "Okay, but I mean, for a joyride or something?"

"The owner denies it ever left his property that afternoon."

"So, how did he explain the repairs to the front end?" Frustration churned, and she got up to pace behind her desk.

"Says that happened on a weekend drive into the moun-tains. Swerved to miss a deer and bumped into a tree."

"Can you verify that?" Her voice rose in pitch.

A heavy sigh came through the phone. "Unfortunately, no. It doesn't look like he's our guy."

Amelia's throat closed. He didn't believe her. She rubbed her face. "It's the right car, I *swear*. That YODELL plate is burned into my memory."

"I'm sorry, Ms. Jones. We don't have enough to make it stick." The sheriff sounded as frustrated as her. "We will continue other lines of enquiry, though. Hopefully, we will find the culprit."

"Sure. Thanks." Amelia had no energy to even say

goodbye and rang off, tossing her phone on the desk and sinking back into her chair. She dropped her head into her hands with a groan.

"What happened?" Violet came over, concern lacing her voice.

Amelia dragged her face up to meet her friend's. "The weasel who ran down that kid is going to get off scot-free because he covered his tracks well. That's what's happened."

"Oh." Violet winced.

"The police don't trust my memory." Amelia rubbed at her eyes.

Violet chewed on her lip. "Is ... is it possible you remembered wrong?"

Amelia clenched her fists. "Not you too. I know what I saw, and no one is going to tell me otherwise."

"Okay, okay." Violet threw her hands up in a show of surrender.

"I need to call Mud." Amelia stood up again, grabbed her phone and headed outside. Thankfully, the rain had let up and now the sun shone. Steam rose from the paved driveway, bringing the heavy scent of fresh rain. She tapped the call button.

"Hey." Mud's voice sounded flat. Or maybe he was busy working and she'd interrupted him. She heard the clink of tools in the background.

"I hate to tell you this, but owner of the hatchback denies his car was involved."

"What?"

"Mm-hmm. Apparently he has an alibi and everything." Amelia clenched her teeth. She started pacing again.

"No way."

"Yes way. And now Sheriff Thompson thinks I'm making

things up in my head. But, Mud, it's the right car. I'm *sure* it is."

Silence for a moment. "Yeah, I'm sure too. I saw the way it affected you on sight."

Relief surged through. He believed her. "So what do we do?"

"Hmm. Dunno. Let me think about it, okay?"

Amelia's stomach clenched. Goodness, she sounded needy again. "Never mind. I'm sure they'll figure it out." That was better. Try to appear more casual about it. And how about a complete change of subject? "Hey, are we still on for the movies tomorrow?"

"Yep. Session's at seven, yeah?"

"That's right."

"Can I meet you there? I've got a bit going on tomorrow."

Amelia paused. That was a first. But, sure, it was none of her business anyway. She didn't need him to pick her up. Now that Nick was back in town, he was probably more interested in hanging out with him. "Sure. See you then."

———

MUD STILL CHURNED over the fact Nick fell asleep on him last night. Lying beneath a car, he put extra force into tightening nuts as he worked. Anger pulsated through him. His best friend didn't seem to care that he had exposed his soul. Mud clenched his teeth and pulled the wrench tighter again. Sure, he might have been jet lagged, so why didn't he say so before inviting conversation? Guilt mixed with his ire. Nick had no idea how bad things were, so why would he behave with any kind of sensitivity? Mud knew his anger was unfair.

Not that his heart cared about fair. And now Amelia wanted his help again. Didn't any of them see *he* was the one who needed help? Even if it was the hardest thing on earth for him to do—ask for help—didn't people have a sense about these things? Why didn't someone ask him if *he* was okay? Not in the trivial, I-don't-really-care-about-the-answer way, but genuinely want to hear him.

Dude. Be honest. If someone asked him, he would probably say he was fine. So, what then? Right now, he didn't want to face Nick. After work he would hit the gym for a few hours. He didn't want to get home until Nick was asleep. And that shouldn't be too late.

Mud shifted his thoughts to Amelia. He both craved seeing her and wanted to stay away from her at the same time. He wouldn't stand her up for the movie. He'd promised he wouldn't, and she was worth every minute, even if it meant he was uncomfortable. Hopefully, he could hide his grief a little longer. He didn't want to ruin it for her. But the length of a movie was as long as he would risk right now. Thank goodness it wasn't some soppy tear-jerker.

What were they going to do about the car? Amelia was certain she was on the right track and Mud truly believed her. Someone else must have used YODELL's car. So why wouldn't he admit that? Surely, the owner would recognize the heinous nature of the crime and want to turn them in. Unless … unless he was protecting them.

Mud slid out from beneath the car and lowered the jacks. Perhaps some good old-fashioned stalking was in order. The idea brought lightness to his thoughts. He'd start tonight and avoid Nick at the same time.

Once he'd finished work and worn himself out at the gym, Mud drove to the neighborhood where the hatchback lived. He parked across the road from the owner, Andy O'Dell's address. It was the name Steve from the body shop had given him with the details.

Mud didn't want to arouse suspicion, so if this didn't work tonight he'd have to reconsider his plans. For now, he watched and noted this guy's movements. He hoped he'd learn something that could give him an opportunity to meeting the man.

Problem was, after the last few late nights and excessive workouts, he was tired. Bone weary. Even a few cans of energy drink didn't help. Without someone else to talk to, staying awake would be a challenge. He looked around him and all he had was the notebook he'd brought to write YODELL's patterns. With a shrug, he opened it and put his pen to the page. He started with a letter to his mum, apologizing for not coming home after Griff died. She deserved an explanation after all.

But that meant the memories flooded in again. Griff's broken body. The trauma of sorting out what to do when your brother dies in a foreign country, in the middle of nowhere. Images of blood and flashing lights passed through his mind. Flames of fire seemed to lick at his heels.

And then came the screams.

"Help! Help us! Please." A woman's voice. Desperate. From inside the fire. Inside the house.

Mud looked down at the hose in his hand. Water dribbled from the nozzle and he panicked. It should be a powerful burst, enough to douse the flames. He frantically glanced around at the other firefighters. "There," he pointed. "Direct the water there. We have to save them."

But it was as though no one heard him. No-one saw him. And the women and children continued to scream. Wild with despair, Mud threw down his hose and raced into the house, a wall of heat crashing into him as he entered. Where were they? He couldn't see through the smoke and flames.

"I'm here," he yelled. "Call out to me."

"Here!" A response came but the direction remained unclear. Which way should he go? Left or right? Left or right? He charged left, hoping he headed to the family. He checked through one door and another, but nothing moved. There was no one. The screams came again, behind him this time. Had he missed them? He turned around but fire surrounded him with no space to move. Panic took hold as he charged into the inferno.

Mud jolted awake, his face covered in sweat and tears, panting for breath, and his heart rate raced as though he'd been on the treadmill at top speed. *Again*. How many times did he have to relive that tragedy? He concentrated on his breathing, slowing it and calming himself, using the techniques he'd learned.

The nightmare was always worse than the actual events. A fire station chaplain had told him it was the brain's way of processing trauma. Mud wondered if it would ever finish processing. He ached all over, stiff both from the tension in his body and from sleeping in the car. He glanced at the time. Three A.M. Andy O'Dell's car remained in the driveway and all the lights were off. Mud wouldn't learn anything tonight. He drove home and snuck inside, making a beeline for bed.

When he woke the next morning, his head throbbed, but his watch told him it was almost midday. He checked his phone where several messages from Nick waited, some of which he'd ignored yesterday.

Hey man. You okay?

Really sorry I fell asleep on you. Jetlag sucks.

And a couple from this morning.

Wanna hang out today? Skydive? Trail bike? You pick.

Late night, eh, sleepy head?

Then …

Are you mad at me?

Mud groaned. His head hurt too much to explain. Nick would no doubt pester him until he got an answer so he typed a reply.

All good, man. Rain check on today. Not feeling great. Gonna sleep it off.

Nick would probably assume he had a hangover and leave him alone now. Mud pulled the bedcovers up over his head and returned to his slumber.

It was late afternoon before he ventured from the room. Thankfully, both Nick and Manny were out of the house, so he relaxed as he downed some paracetamol, found food to eat and got ready for the movie with Amelia.

He only hoped he didn't look as bedraggled as he felt. As he approached the ticket office he mentally pumped himself up, thrust his shoulders back, and forced a grin. "Hey, Meels." Of course, she had to look gorgeous wearing a dusty brown dress with ankle boots and a headscarf, long beads dangling from her porcelain neck.

"Hey, yourself." Her smile was soft.

Mud thrust his hands into his pockets to keep from touching her, holding her, kissing her cheek.

Amelia led him to the counter and motioned her hand toward the register on the other side. "This is Linyu Foo, but everyone calls him Foo. He's the owner-manager here. We attended college together."

Mud nodded and offered him a smile. "Nice to meet you, Foo."

"And you," he replied. Foo leaned closer over the counter. "Come see me whenever you want to see a movie. I give special discounts to friends and their partners."

"Oh, we're not … um …" Color infused Amelia's cheeks.

"Yeah, I'm just the dude she dragged here so she doesn't look like a complete loner." Mud pretended a yawn.

Amelia turned to face him, eyes wide. "Gee. Thanks. Great friend you are." Her lips twitched, though, showing her amusement.

Foo rolled his eyes like he thought they were down-playing the truth. "Never mind. Discount applied anyway."

"Tell him about this place, Foo," Amelia said with enthusiasm.

"Okay." Foo turned to him. "So, they were planning to demolish this building a few years ago. It had been sitting unused and in disrepair for a long time. I'm a bit of a history buff," he said with a hand on his heart, "so when I heard about it, I went into battle with the council. Thankfully, others in town didn't want to lose our heritage, either. They also fought to get the museum back up and running. Well, the end of it was, I had some inheritance money so I purchased and restored the theater. But in keeping with the heritage feel, we only show old movies—none of the new stuff."

"That's very cool." Mud nodded. "And it works well for those of us who love old movies."

"Do you happen to be one of those?" Foo lifted his brows in question.

Mud placed a finger over his lips. "Shh, don't tell anyone." He turned to Amelia and stuck his elbow out. "Shall we?"

CHAPTER NINE

Did Amelia imagine it or was Mud more subdued than normal? Since buying their tickets and hitting the candy bar, he'd barely said a word. He sat beside her watching the movie in silence. She half expected him to lean over and interrupt with witty comments throughout the screening. But, no. He fixed his eyes straight ahead and only laughed when everyone else laughed. She frequently slid her gaze sideways to check on him, as she did now.

"What?"

Oops. He noticed this time. She might as well express her concern so she turned to him properly and whispered. "Are you okay?"

His eyes burned into hers with intensity for a moment but then his expression softened. "I'm fine. A bit tired is all." He turned back to the screen.

A few minutes later when she reached for some popcorn, their hands brushed as he moved to do the same. Amelia jerked her hand away as awareness shot through her at the brief contact. She rubbed her hands together in her lap trying to still the flutter in her heart, wondering when she should repeat her attempt for popcorn. She didn't dare look his way, worried she'd find him laughing at her. Or worse, frowning.

It was a while before Amelia found the courage to get a handful of popcorn again. This time, it was as though he was waiting for her. As soon as her hand neared the box his fingers slid over her wrist and covered her hand, holding tight although she jolted and tried to pull away. She intended to look at him with a frown but his lips curved up softly and his thumb caressed the back of her hand.

Heart in overdrive and heat flooding her face, she tried to return her focus to the screen. He wasn't teasing her, he was holding her hand. Which was quite wonderful, but …

He let her go and whispered. "Sorry."

Why would he be sorry? Her hand was cold now that his warmth was gone. Should she tell him it was okay? That she didn't mind holding hands after all? Amelia closed her eyes tight for a few seconds. No, she hadn't wanted this. She must remember how he'd treated Bree. He wasn't a stayer, especially since he would go back to Australia after Nick and Vi's wedding. This … whatever it was … would have to remain at friendship, nothing more.

Finally, the movie finished and they moved outside toward the parking lot. It was probably a good thing they came in separate cars as her emotions were all a-jumble right now. Shoving her attraction and the accompanying longing aside, Amelia put on a chirpy voice. "So, what's the plan?"

"Plan for what?" Mud seemed genuinely unaware of her meaning.

"YODELL. Do you have any ideas?" She explained.

"Aha. Oui," he said in a French accent as he tapped his temple. "We must figure out what Mr. O'Dell is hiding."

Amelia rolled her eyes. "You're not Hercule Poirot, you know."

Mud chuckled and shoved his hands in his pockets. "No. But I *would* like to learn the truth. For your peace of mind."

It was hard to hide her grin at that. "Aww, thanks." Her heart threatened to go on a rampage again but she shoved it down. "So, what have you come up with?"

Mud rubbed his forehead. "Nothing exactly legal," he mumbled.

Amelia stopped dead in her tracks.

"It's okay." Mud put his hands out toward her. "I'm not gonna get myself in trouble. I'm just watching him. See if there's anywhere he goes where I might *accidentally* meet him, if you know what I mean."

"No, Mud." Amelia shook her head. "Don't put yourself at risk for my sake. We'll leave it to the police. It's their job, anyway."

Mud stepped closer, his eyes fixed on hers. "You worried about me, Meels?" There was an edge to his voice and his hands wrapped around hers.

Amelia glanced down at their hands but didn't pull away this time. "I don't want to be responsible if you get caught spying on him."

"That would be my decision, not your responsibility." Mud didn't shift his gaze from hers.

"I'm not worth the trouble, really," she whispered.

Mud's eyes did that intense search of all her features again. "What if I think you are?"

Oh, Lord, he was going to kiss her. And this time she didn't want to stop him. Words stuck in her throat and she swallowed. "Do you?" she murmured as he leaned even closer.

She closed her eyes as his cologne filled her senses. One

of his hands released hers and moved to her jawline, sending thrills through her. His other arm encircled her waist, drawing her in. She slid her hands to his chest where the thrum of his heart beat beneath her touch.

"Yes." His breath caressed her cheek and then warmth as his lips met hers, sweet and gentle at first and becoming more ardent as she responded.

Everything disappeared in that moment, including her sanity, as she allowed herself to enjoy this pleasure, this desire. But after a minute of sheer bliss, reality knocked on her heart like some unwanted harbinger. This was Mud. The player. The breaker of hearts.

She pushed against his chest to end the kiss, but couldn't bring herself to tell him she didn't want this. She pressed a hand over her lips, which still burned, and stared at him.

"Sorry." Mud's eyes were wide as he backed away from her.

Sorry. The same as when he held her hand in the cinema. Was he fighting this attraction as much as she was? Right now, she didn't want to know the answer to that question, or explore what had just happened. "We should ... I should go." Amelia half turned towards her car.

Mud shoved his hands deep in his pockets again. "Yep. Yeah. Okay." He jerked his chin down in a brief nod. "See ya 'round." He turned and hurried away.

Amelia fumbled with her keys as she unlocked her Mini and sank into the driver's seat. She closed her eyes and held on to the steering wheel, still trembling from Mud's touch. She had sworn to herself that she would never go there, but with a few romantic words she'd caved like a sandcastle beneath the waves. Amelia smashed her palms against the steering wheel in frustration then started the car and headed home.

But that kiss, though. *Oh, my goodness.* She wouldn't forget that in a hurry.

———

WHAT AN IDIOT. Mud was unable to stay still. Back at Nick's place, he indulged in a whirlwind of housecleaning. Sweeping, mopping, vacuuming, dishes and a load of laundry. Who cared that it was nearly midnight? He had to keep busy. Get rid of this energy.

Hadn't he told himself he couldn't afford an attachment right now? So why the heck did he kiss Amelia? It wasn't merely because he found her attractive and intriguing. He wanted to feel something that wasn't pain and heartache for a change. And man, did he feel it. The sparks that flew reminded him of cracker night in the Northern Territory. The one day of the year when Territorians bought and set off fireworks legally. Explosive, loud and fun, but also a little dangerous.

He could get burned by her. Or she by him. She had taken off pretty quickly after. Was that because he'd scared her off? Moved too fast? She had said she only wanted to be friends. Mud ran the vacuum over the same piece of carpet again with more force than required.

"Bro, what are you doing?"

Mud hadn't seen Nick come in. He must have returned from his date with Violet. Far out, now he'd have to confront that problem.

"What does it look like?" Mud frowned at him.

Nick rolled his eyes and laughed. "I can see you're vacuuming, but dude, it's the middle of the night."

"So?" Mud couldn't keep the antagonism from his voice.

Nick walked over and put a hand on his shoulder, eyes showing concern. "Mud, are you okay?"

The question he'd wanted to be asked. The question Amelia asked and he'd answered with a partial truth. The question he didn't want to answer right now. "I'm *fine*."

"Really?" Nick's face said he didn't believe him.

"Really." He forced his mouth to turn up.

Nick rubbed his face. "Okay. Well, tomorrow arvo, you and me," he waved his hand back and forth between them, "we're going trail biking. No arguments."

Mud's stomach clenched. That was the last thing he wanted to do. But he realized he really wanted some time to hang out with Nick, even if his so-called best friend fell asleep while he spilled his guts. "Sure. Tomorrow arvo."

Nick walked towards his room, flinging words over his shoulder. "And go to bed. You'll be keeping Manny awake with that racket."

Fair enough. Not that he hadn't thought of it before, but his angst had outweighed his courtesy. He probably needed to sleep too. That might help his state of mind. *If* he even slept. He packed the cleaning equipment away, took a quick shower, and hopped into bed.

Problem was, Amelia kept floating back into his thoughts. The sensation of her lips on his, the way she responded. Oh, yes. She had kissed him back. He didn't imagine the pull between them. Still, he wasn't in a right state to dwell on any potential relationship.

Damn you, Griff. It was his brother's fault his head was a mess. If Griff hadn't gone and died, Mud would be fine. Well, better than a month ago at any rate. Guilt assailed him and he tossed around in the bed. He shouldn't be angry with his brother. It was an accident. Pure dumb luck. So, why was he so down?

Sleep finally claimed him in the early hours and he didn't wake until Nick knocked on the bedroom door. "You ready to go, mate?"

Mud jerked into a sitting position, rubbing his face. "Dude. Sorry. Just woke up."

Nick opened the door and grinned at him. "All good. I'll give you five minutes."

Mud threw his pillow across the room but Nick ducked out of the way with a laugh.

"Nah. Jokes bro. Take your time."

An hour later they were in Nick's new ute—or pickup as he told Mud it was supposed to be called.

"Pfft. I'm still gonna call it a ute."

"Of course you are."

"Where are we going?" Mud asked, glancing over his shoulder at the two trail bikes in the back.

"There are some great tracks up in the mountains near the ski lodge. It's all used for skiing in winter, but in summer—"

"Hiking and riding. Got it."

Half an hour later, Nick pulled into the ski lodge parking lot and they unloaded the trail bikes.

"You got a helmet for me?" Mud asked. His heart already hammered in his chest. He tried to tell himself that trail bikes differed completely from mountain bikes but it didn't seem to make much difference. In fact, motorbikes were probably more dangerous.

"Of course." Nick scoffed. "Safety one-oh-one." With those words he grabbed two helmets from the ute and handed one to Mud.

Mud quickly pulled the helmet over his head and closed the visor. He didn't want Nick to see the anxiety on his face.

Nick mounted his bike and revved it up. "You ready?" He looked over his shoulder.

"Yep." Mud thought Nick wouldn't hear his weak reply but Nick took off up the path away from the lodge.

Mud started his bike and followed. Slowly. His breath came short and rapid and his heart raced uncontrollably. At the first turn in the track he faltered, the back wheel slid sideways and Mud yelled in panic. He braked, got off the bike, thew it to the ground and stalked away from it. He hadn't even lost his balance but that was it. He couldn't do it. Could not sit on that thing and see images of Griff flying over the handlebars with every twist and turn of the path. Suddenly, the helmet suffocated him and he tried to undo it and yank it off, but his fingers fumbled.

Nick's bike revved behind him as he returned.

"Get it off! Get it off me," he screamed.

"Dude. Calm down." Nick held him still. "What? You got a bee in your bonnet?" He laughed as the helmet finally came free.

"Don't laugh at me." Mud shoved him with both hands, full force in the chest, and Nick lost his balance, landing on his butt, shock all over his face. "Don't you dare laugh at me!"

Mud grabbed at his own chest, tearing at his leathers which were now tight and as suffocating as the helmet. "I can't breathe. I can't breathe."

"Woah, Mud." Nick scrambled to his feet again, a hand stretched out before him. "What's wrong?"

Mud could only gasp and groan, still trying to remove his jacket in a frenzy. His whole body was in overdrive. He was going to die on a bike trail in the middle of nowhere, just like his brother.

"Is it an asthma attack?" Nick looked truly worried now. "What can I do?"

"I ... can't ... breathe." Tears ran down his cheeks now. "Griff ... *died*." Mud collapsed to the ground, his strength gone, head spinning.

Nick stood as a stone for what seemed an eternity, but was probably a few seconds, and then kneeled beside him. "He died? Oh my ... He *died*? Mud. I'm so sorry. So, so sorry." His eyes were glassy, but he swallowed, blinking away his tears. "And you're having a panic attack."

Understatement of the year. And one he couldn't control right now. He nodded, gasping.

"Alright." Nick grabbed his forearms. "Look at me and follow my breathing."

Mud nodded again.

"In. Hold it. Out. Count to five. Come on. You can do it." Nick coached him and repeated it until Mud's breathing finally slowed and his heart rate came down as well. Then all that remained was grief, which left him sobbing like a little babe.

"I can't ride the bike, Nick. I can't." Mud wiped at his tears with the heel of his palm, frustrated at his weakness.

"Hey, if I'd known, I never would've suggested it." Nick shook his head, face grim. "I take it Griff died on the mountain bike."

Mud nodded. "I tried to tell you the other night."

Understanding dawned on Nick's face. "When I fell asleep."

Mud nodded again.

"Man, I'm so sorry. You have no idea how sorry I am. I figured something was up with you, but this? I never would have guessed." Nick shifted to sit beside him in the dust, knees bent, arms draped over them, head hanging low.

It took a moment to realize Nick was crying, too, albeit quietly. "Nick?"

His friend lifted a hurt gaze to him. "Why didn't you tell me? Griff was my friend, too. I would have come to the funeral. Been there for you and your family."

Mud looked at the ground, guilt and shame piling up. "I … I haven't talked to anyone. Not even Mum. Not since they flew his body home. I didn't go to the funeral either. It was too much."

"What?" Nick rubbed the back of his neck. "Dude, that's not healthy."

And that was the truth. Keeping it all locked up was doing him in. Maybe that all needed to change.

CHAPTER TEN

Violet's words kept intruding into Amelia's thoughts, now partnering with her yearning to be loved. The words that Jesus loved her. That she could depend on God. Even if Mud found her attractive, all accounts declared he was unreliable for any kind of permanent relationship. How was it that a few short weeks ago she thought his carefree, untangled lifestyle was what she wanted? If she admitted the truth, she wanted to settle down and establish a real connection with someone who loved and cared for her.

Until the hit-and-run she'd thought she never needed anyone but it had become clear that, perhaps, that might not be the truth. Not something she ever thought she'd admit. Yet, the idea of someone else depending on her for *their* needs still terrified her.

With the realization of her growing need and Violet's earnest assurances rolling around in her mind, Amelia decided to visit Violet's church again. Give it another try. This time not looking to see which guy might be suitable, but rather being open—to listen to what they were teaching.

She snuck in after the evening service started at Trinity Lakes Community Church. When she spotted Nick and Vi she made sure she sat directly behind them, right at the back so they wouldn't see her. Not until after, at least. She didn't want her friend to assume this would be a permanent thing, in case it wasn't. Amelia was merely curious, that's all.

She settled in and listened as someone made announcements about things planned in the coming weeks. There was certainly a happy community vibe in the place from the laughter that rang out as the emcee bantered. How long had it been since she'd experienced that kind of family atmosphere? Not since Mom left, really. And she had experienced a shadow of it with Mud the other week. Might she find belonging here, in a church of all places?

The minister got up to speak and straight away it was as though the rest of the room disappeared. Was this man speaking to her? She glanced around. Who'd have told him about her? Violet? Nick? Surely not. But the man started talking about love and what real love looked like. He read words from the Bible that appeared up on the screen.

"First Corinthians, chapter thirteen, verses four to seven," he read. "Love is patient. Love is kind. It does not envy, it does not boast, it is not proud. It does not dishonor others, it is not self-seeking, it is not easily angered, it keeps no record of wrongs. Love does not delight in evil but rejoices with the truth. It always protects, always trusts, always hopes, always perseveres."

The minister took his glasses off and placed them on the pulpit, then looked up and around at the audience. "The word 'love' is bandied about these days like it means nothing. For example, 'I love ice cream. I love my car.' But this isn't what real love is about. *Real* love, God's love, the love he wants us to show others, is all about honoring others above ourselves. It's not about me and what I want.

"Jesus told us in the gospels that we are to love our neighbor as ourselves. We therefore should treat each other as per the Corinthians' definition. Be patient and kind. Not selfish. Pretty much opposite to what the world says. We hear it often enough. 'The most important person is you.' But it's not true.

"Romans twelve, ten says, 'Be devoted to one another in love. Honor one another *above* yourselves.' If we were to always consider the other person's best, rather than our own, what do you think the world would look like?"

Murmurs of agreement hummed throughout the room. Is this what she'd been missing all this time? Moms and dads were supposed to love their kids, right? But Mom's leaving wasn't acting for Pa's best or for Amelia's either. And Pa making her meet all his needs without taking care of her? That wasn't love. Not really. Not that Amelia thought she was perfect or anything. If she never received proper love, how was she supposed to learn how to love? Was that the answer to this inescapable yearning?

And if God required that kind of selfless love from people, didn't that mean He loved that way? Certainly, it would hold little credibility if he didn't. She refocused on the preacher just in time for him to say, "But God demonstrates his own love for us in this: While we were still sinners, Christ died for us."

Amelia's mouth dropped open. Did he hear her thoughts? She sucked in her breath and glanced around the room again. Or was it … *God* … who heard her? Was He here? Nerves churned in her stomach. This was too weird.

She looked back to the front to see the preacher inviting people to come forward and open their hearts to Jesus.

Amelia wished the floor might open up and swallow her. He was staring at her, she was sure of it. More uncomfortable than she had even been with Mud's advances, Amelia grabbed her purse and fled the building.

Amelia didn't want to go home, though. She wanted to process everything she'd heard and thought. And the only person she knew to do that with was Violet, so she drove straight to the Country Club Estate to wait until her friend came home. Having her own key for the office, Amelia let herself in, made herself a mocha and sat on the chic lounge.

Thankfully, it wasn't too long until an engine sound came up the drive.

"Hello? Amelia." Violet came in, her eyes searching before she spotted her. "I saw your car out front and the lights on. Is everything alright?"

Nick appeared behind her, a hint of sadness in his eyes. "Hey Amelia."

"Um, yeah," Amelia mumbled. "I wanted to have a chat, that's all." She glanced at Nick. "Sorry, did you have plans? I can go." She moved to get up.

"No, it's fine." He put a hand out to stop her. "I need to get back to Mud, anyway."

Violet swiveled to face him. "Yeah, you should check on him, hon." She stroked his arm.

"Why does Mud need checking?" Amelia asked, still standing.

Nick scratched at his beard and winced. "His brother died." He swallowed. "Sorry. We were all close."

"When? Today?" Dismay filled Amelia and her heart ached for her new friend.

"Umm." Words seemed to catch in his throat. "Over a month ago, actually."

Violet wrapped her arms around Nick's waist and rubbed his back. "Tragic accident," she said to Amelia.

Amelia stared at them, first one, then the other, disbelief making her gasp. "He never said."

Nick shook his head. "Nope. Not even to his best friend. I only found out today."

Amelia sank back into the sofa, unsure what to make of this news. While Violet saw Nick out, she traced her mind back over all the times she'd shared with Mud. Not once did he hint that he'd lost a brother. No. Wait. That time at the pizzeria, when she'd asked him about his family, and he suddenly acted weird. And the look on his face at the gym. Oh yeah. The signs were definitely there.

Why would he keep all this to himself? Wasn't she supposed to be his friend, too?

Violet came back into the room and sat down with a heavy sigh. "So, what did you want to talk about?"

Amelia dragged her eyes up to meet her friend's. Why was she here again? Oh, yes. The love thing. She shook her head. "Never mind. Nothing important. Tell me what happened with Mud's brother."

Violet spent the next half hour going over the story as she'd heard it from Nick. How Mud had a massive panic attack on the bike trails and Nick had to work hard to stop him hyperventilating. And after that, the truth came out.

"What I don't get is why he didn't tell anyone." Amelia still wrestled with that part.

Violet shrugged. "I don't know. Some people struggle to express their emotions. Perhaps they think it makes them appear weak."

"Right, so the hero-first-responder doesn't want to look like the one who needs rescue." Amelia pressed her lips together.

"Maybe." Violet reached a hand out to her. "We're speculating here. Why don't you ask him yourself?"

"Why?" Amelia frowned. "It's not like we're close or anything."

Except they kind of were, if that kiss was any indication. Or potentially heading that way, if she allowed it.

Vi lifted her hands in surrender. "Sorry. You seem concerned about him."

Amelia averted her eyes. "Well, I'm not. I was just curious, that's all." She stood up. "I probably should go. See you tomorrow?"

Vi's mouth curved upward. "You know you will."

Outside Violet's house Amelia released a long breath. Was her interest in Mud beginning to show that much? Last year she'd deflected any suspicion with ease. If she wasn't careful Violet would have it all figured out soon. Of course, if things progressed with Mud, she'd have to tell her friend, eventually. But that wouldn't happen. She shook off those sentiments once again. What kind of friend kept such a tragic secret to themselves?

———

MUD WALKED along the streets of Trinity Lakes sipping on a bottle of bourbon. He'd probably walked for hours. He'd lost track of time. Part of him was glad Nick finally understood about Griff, but the dam of his grief had broken, unleashing an unstoppable flood. He had to stop walking frequently and let the tears flow. Well, sobs, to put it bluntly, which he tried to swallow with the liquor. It was hard to put one foot in front of the other when his feet were blurred by blinding tears. Plus, there was the embarrassment of publicly crying like a baby. He'd hidden in several corners and bushes in the last couple of hours.

He kind of felt sorry for Nick, too. Mud was ashamed he hadn't found the courage to tell him before now. Hadn't thought of how that might affect him. Hadn't considered Nick might want to grieve with him. Mud was a lousy friend. He didn't deserve the grace Nick offered, especially knowing he grieved as well. Which made him remember Mum, and how his actions would've caused her anguish as well. A lousy friend and a lousy son. And probably a lousy boyfriend for the trifecta.

No. He backtracked on that thought. There was no specific agreement between him and Amelia, even if they'd shared an amazing kiss. And yet, previous girlfriends would probably say he was no good. Either way, Amelia must see him as a terrible person by now.

Pangs squeezed his heart again as Griff's face appeared in his memory, and he took another swig of the drink. If only he could talk to his brother one more time. Griff was always good with the girl stuff. A lot more liberal in his views on how to treat a woman than Nick. Mud rubbed his face and groaned as guilt twisted again. *Please, please, don't make me think ill of my brother.* He didn't know who or what he was talking to. His head? His heart? God?

Mud gazed at his surroundings. He'd walked right to the bridge that spanned Lake Wainscott. He kept going, not ready to turn around yet, unwilling to face another sleepless night of tossing and turning. There were too many questions, too much self-recrimination, too much doubt and sorrow.

A red truck approached him slowly, flashing lights and sounding the horn cheerfully. Oh, that must be Brandon. He lifted a hand to wave as his fellow mechanic passed. There were so many friendly people in this town. It reminded him of some of the outback communities in Australia.

At the pinnacle of the bridge, Mud stopped to gaze over the edge at the moonlight reflecting over the water of the lake. So peaceful. Much like the facade he'd tried to portray, but there were probably currents and eddies under the surface as turbulent as his thoughts.

He hoisted himself up onto the barrier and stood tall. Below, dark waters. Above, dark sky. He tipped his head back, lifting the bottle to his lips again. A myriad stars broke the darkness of night. Was one of those stars Griff? Was there a heaven up there where people went after they died? He no longer wanted to believe there was nothing after this life. Nothing to look forward to. Nothing to strive for. All that nothingness made life meaningless.

Mud used his sleeve to wipe his eyes and nose once again. God help him, he wanted meaning. He walked back and forth on the concrete barrier like it was a balancing beam, adrenaline thrilling through him every time he swayed. He chuckled and then dissolved into tears again. "Where are you, Griff?" he called into the night. "Where are you?"

The crunch of tires on pavement met his ears and he and turned to see Nick's ute pulling up. "Hey, Nick." He held up the bottle like a salute.

"Mud, please." Nick approached slowly. "Get down."

"Why?" Mud frowned at him. "It's nice up here. Great view. You should come up and see."

"You don't need to do this." Nick seemed desperate.

Mud looked from his friend to the barrier on which he stood, to the calm waters below and back before realization hit. "Oh, do you think—? I'm not—Don't be stupid, bro."

"Huh?"

"It's not even high enough." Mud pointed down toward

the water. "I'm just having some fun. Come and join me." Mud sat down on the barrier with his legs dangling toward the water and patted the concrete beside him.

Mud drank from his bottle again, and it was a minute before he finally recognized the shuffle of footsteps and Nick's grunt as his friend hoisted himself up.

"How'd you find me?"

"I've been calling everyone in your phone—which you left behind. I was worried about you." Nick perched next to him on the barrier. "Brandon told me he saw you here."

"Right."

"So, what's going on?" Nick asked.

Mud pointed to the sky with the hand that held the bottle. "Do you think Griff's up there?"

Nick scratched his beard and pinched his nose. "I don't know," he mumbled.

"Why not?" Mud glared at him. "And what about those kids that died in the fire? Are they up there?"

Nick wore a pained look, but before he opened his mouth, Mud continued.

"Where's Griff, Nick? I want to know where he is?" Stupid tears ran out of his eyes again.

Nick tugged at his arm. "Come on. Let's get you home. We can talk about it after you've had some rest."

"Promise?" Mud pulled his arm away but swung his legs over to the roadside anyway. "Promise me you'll tell me where Griff is." He swiped at his wet cheeks again.

"I promise." Nick helped him jump down and led him to the car. "Come on, mate."

The next morning, Mud woke with a splitting headache and a weight as heavy as lead in his stomach. He called the auto-shop and left a message on the answering machine, apologizing he wouldn't be there. When he dragged himself out of bed to find some paracetamol, he discovered Nick still at home.

"Aren't you supposed to be at work or something?" Mud grunted.

"Well, apart from the fact it's Memorial Day, right now you're my top priority." Nick's lips pressed in a straight line. "How are you this morning?"

Mud gave him an expletive in reply, then gulped down a glass of water.

"I figured as much." Nick rose and entered the kitchen. "Here, sit down. I'll make you a coffee and toast."

"I'm not hungry," Mud grumbled, but sat down anyway.

"Even if I have Vegemite?" Nick winked.

Mud grunted again. "Okay. You win."

While Nick worked in the kitchen, Mud tried to remember the night before. Had he made a fool of himself? Too much blubbering, that's for sure. And then he remembered something Nick said. When his friend placed a coffee next to him, he stared up at him.

"You said Griff wasn't in heaven?" Drat it. Why did his eyes have to leak again? "Why would you say that?"

With a deep huff, Nick sat down at the table across from him. "That's not what I said."

"You did. You said you didn't know."

"That's a far cry from stating your brother isn't in heaven." Nick's brows lowered.

Mud blinked at him, not comprehending. "I thought you knew this stuff."

Nick released another sigh. "The truth is, I would never claim to know where Griff's soul has gone. A man's salvation is between him and God." He glanced at the table and scratched at a dirt mark. "But I am confident that *you* can know where you'll go when you die."

Mud sipped at the coffee. There was something comforting about a hot drink in times like these. "Is it real? Heaven, I mean?"

"The Bible says it is, and I believe the Bible is the word of God," Nick answered. "And there are plenty of stories of people who say they've been there and come back."

"NDEs, you mean?"

"Yes, near-death experiences." Nick's mouth curved up a little. "That and those who've had an encounter with Jesus. I've heard enough to believe."

Mud stared at the dark liquid in his mug. "So, if it's real, how do you get there?"

Nick's smile grew. "Well, that's all about a relationship with Jesus. The Bible says that 'God so loved the world, He gave His only son, that whoever believes in Him will not perish but have eternal life.'"

Mud glanced at him. "That's it? Just believe?"

"Well, it's more than believing, because once you realize who He is, you want to know Him more and live for Him."

"Realize who He is?"

Nick placed both hands flat on the table. "If you're open to it, I'd suggest reading the gospel of John. You'll learn heaps about who Jesus is in there." His lips twitched and his eyes sparked.

Mud frowned at him. "Don't get too excited. I haven't agreed to anything yet."

CHAPTER ELEVEN

"Only two months to go." Violet's sing-song voice greeted Amelia on Monday morning. "I'm going to need you to help me finalize a bunch of wedding plans. Nick's spending the day with Mud and is happy for us to decide without him. I'll text him anything important, of course."

Even though it was Memorial Day they'd organized to work on Vi's wedding, but flowers and fripperies were the last thing on Amelia's mind. Despite her distracted state she sucked in a breath, put on a bright smile and clapped. "Yay."

Once they started working, though, Amelia soon enjoyed the process, constantly noticing that her own choices would be far different from Vi's. Her friend chose arum lilies where Amelia preferred roses any day. Vi had booked stretch limousines, but Amelia would probably choose a horse and cart. Another difference was the cake. Vi opted for traditional fruit cake, and Amelia mentally noted that chocolate would be better.

As she suspected, Nick and Vi had to find a compromise

with Mr. and Mrs. Reynolds. They had eventually agreed on a simple outdoor ceremony in a garden setting by Lake Wainscott, but the reception would be no-expense-spared luxury.

"Daddy's being so generous. It's a little overwhelming," Vi told her. "He not only offered to fly Nick's parents over from Australia but all his sisters and their partners as well. Plus, he's leased an entire house for them all to stay in."

"Wow. Nick must be so excited." Amelia put her hands on her cheeks.

"That's an understatement." Vi giggled. "Now, can you check that we've put the appointment for Nick's fitting in the diary? It was early July, if I remember correctly."

Amelia checked both the online calendar and the paper diary. "Yes, it says tux fitting on the third." Another unconventional choice Amelia would make. Tuxedos were nice, but she fancied her man in full Victorian evening wear, complete with long coat and cravat. An image of Mud in such attire popped into her mind, making her stomach quiver. No, no. She must stop thinking about him.

That was a tall order. He was constantly on her mind for two reasons. Firstly, her heart went out to him as he must be grieving his brother. Then there was the question of whether he was going to continue the secret investigation of YODELL. But would it be appropriate for her to contact him? And if she did, should she text or phone? She needed to do something. It would seem heartless if she didn't, wouldn't it?

"Just do it, Amelia." Violet's voice came from across the room, startling her.

"Do what?" How was it everyone seemed to read the thoughts in her head?

"Make the call. Send the text. Whatever is making you pick up and put down your phone repeatedly."

Seriously? She had noticed that? Amelia huffed.

"What are you thinking?" Vi turned on her chair and held her in an intense gaze.

"Mud was really helpful when that accident happened. Shouldn't I reciprocate or something? Or is that too presumptuous?" Perhaps he didn't want to hear from her. He hadn't been honest with her when he had the chance. She'd asked him straight out if he was okay several times and yet, nothing.

"I'm sure he wouldn't mind knowing someone else is thinking about him. Especially after what happened last night."

Amelia drew her brows together. "What happened last night? I thought Nick found him."

Vi put two fingers over her lips for a moment, as if deciding what to say next. "Nick only had time to send a brief text to stop everyone worrying. I heard the full story this morning. Mud's not in a good way. He could use a friend … or five … right now. I don't see a problem in reaching out." She shrugged. "If he doesn't respond, that's on him."

It was all very well to say, "that's on him", but Amelia knew she wouldn't be immune to him ignoring her reaching out. There was a very real chance of rejection. "Alright. I'll think about it," she said out loud. And by think about it, she meant she would do it, but not this second. She waited until they took a break, then took her coffee outside and sat on a bench in the front garden overlooking the lake. So pretty with a summer haze over the scene.

Hey, just wanted to see how you're doing. I heard about your brother. So sorry for your loss. Are you ok?

It was a good five minutes before a reply came in.

Thanks, Meels. Yeah, doing ok. Guess where I am?

Amelia sat up a little straighter and re-read the message.

It seemed he didn't want to talk about the revelations of the last couple of days. That both annoyed and hurt. So much for friendship. Part of her didn't even want to bother replying.

No idea. Where?

Staking out Andy O'Dell with Nick.

YODELL? Are you crazy? And now you've got Nick involved?

Amelia chewed on her lip. Why would he pursue this when he needed to sort through his grief, and when it might get him in trouble, or worse? What if Andy O'Dell was dangerous? It was unbelievable to think Nick would agree to something that might be illegal—if Andy O'Dell discovered them and charged them with stalking.

It's all good. We're just taking notes. Looks like he's a tutor of some kind. Students coming and going all day.

Ok. How does that help?

Not sure yet.

Amelia had exhausted this thread of conversation and her mind returned to her original reason for contacting him.

I wish you'd told me.

What? That I was coming here? I told you, you're worth it. Besides, I wanna see this guy face the consequences of his actions.

Amelia's insides quivered as the memory of his kiss resurfaced. But how did he say and do stuff like that one minute, and the next shut down from important things? Well, she wouldn't let him divert her again.

About your brother. You could have told me at the restaurant the other night.

Another five minutes passed before her phone pinged with his reply.

You're right. I'm sorry. Can we talk about it later? It's too hard right now. A couple of broken heart emojis and flooding tears followed.

Amelia clenched her teeth as she typed back. *You want me to give you some space?*

This time the response was immediate. *Thanks for understanding.*

Yes, she understood but disappointment swept in anyway. On the one hand, he fought for justice with Amelia in mind, while on the other, he completely shut her out. What did she expect? They'd been hanging out for barely two weeks. It wasn't as though she had any kind of claim on him. So why did her heart feel so bruised?

Amelia took her empty mug inside and returned to sit with Violet.

"No good?" Vi must have picked up on her dampened spirits.

"He wants to be left alone," Amelia mumbled as she rifled through her folio.

Violet offered a grim smile. "Give him time. He'll come around."

Amelia nodded, but still she wondered. Maybe it was better if he didn't come around. All she did when she was with him was fight attraction. Maybe, like Violet had said, God brought him into her life for that brief season where she needed help, and now he was gone again. So why couldn't she find peace with that?

"Hey, girlfriend."

Amelia looked up to see Violet's eyebrows wiggling.

"What have you got planned for my hen's night?"

Amelia smiled at that. "Wouldn't you like to know?"

"That's why I asked."

"Well, it's a secret." So secret, she hadn't planned it yet. *Goodness.* Where had her mind been that she'd forgotten to organize a special day for her best friend? No prizes guessing the answer to that. But it was an excellent idea to distract her from obsessing about Mud.

Amelia spent the rest of the afternoon searching the internet for ideas on what to do for a bachelorette party. After much research, she decided on a spa weekend with Violet and her closest friends in Soap Lake. A few minutes later, she'd booked reservations for the Fourth of July weekend. They would spoil Vi rotten for a few days—it was no less than she deserved.

———

MUD NEEDED to make a decision where Amelia was concerned. No matter how many times he'd told himself he shouldn't entangle her in his world—especially not now—it didn't stop his heart from skipping a beat or three every time he thought of her. He'd never met anyone like her. Never been enamored so completely before. More than physical, this attraction encompassed her character, interests, personality—everything. Despite being quiet and bookish she had a quirky, dry sense of humor and similar tastes to him. And when she relaxed she was heaps of fun.

This wasn't something to be ignored. She might be his soul-mate. Was it time to hang up his no-strings-attached boots? If only he wasn't so messed up in his head right now. What if his longing for her was all part of his breakdown and he was imagining the depth of their connection?

And now he'd promised he'd talk with her properly about everything. His stomach clenched at the thought. Sharing his grief with Nick was one thing. He was safe—well safe-ish—having been friends since they were in primary school. But putting his heart out there for Amelia, being vulnerable, that was scarier than facing an out-of-control bush fire.

Days passed as he continually put off contacting her to make a time to chat. Even though she had agreed to give him space, he didn't want to leave it too long. She deserved respect. Still, other concerns kept him busy as well. Besides the time Mud volunteered at the auto shop, Nick spent hours listening to him talk through his anguish, for which he was grateful. It helped immensely. Somehow, talking to Nick made the pain diminish even if only by degrees. They often sat parked down the street from Andy O'Dell's house, watching the comings and goings. It was here they had most of their conversations.

Not all their chatter was heavy, thankfully. They also planned Nick's buck's night, completely unlike any buck's night Mud had ever attended. He would never have thought he'd organize something like this, but it was what Nick preferred. They planned to attend the concert of a well-known worship band. Of course, Mud would hatch some kind of prank to play on his mate—that was a given—and Nick eyed him with suspicion every time the topic came up.

"You won't shave my eyebrows off while I'm sleeping or something, will you?"

Mud chuckled. "Dude, you don't drink, and you don't sleep heavy enough. That would be impossible."

"But you're up to something, aren't you?" Nick's eyes narrowed, even though his lips twitched.

"Not telling." Mud shrugged and changed the subject. "Hey, I was thinking." His insides tightened with nerves. "Can I come to church with you this weekend?"

Nick stared at him, then shook his head slightly. "I'm sorry. Can you say that again please?"

"Bro. Are you deaf?"

A slow grin spread across Nick's face. "Nah. I just wanna hear you say it again."

Mud grunted in the back of his throat. "Shut up. But …
can I come? I've been reading the bible a bit, like you said,
and … can I come?"

This time Nick laughed out loud and Mud clenched his
teeth. His friend had been at him for years to come and see
what church was about, so he knew Nick wasn't laughing at
him per se.

"Of course you can come." Nick's eyes gleamed. "I could
hug you right now."

"Calm down." Mud rolled his eyes.

As Sunday approached, Mud thought about changing his
mind. This church thing seemed almost as confronting as
facing Amelia, which was scarier than discovering a king
brown snake coiled in your engine bay. However, his
curiosity about God-stuff overpowered the nagging fear—a
fear which persisted even once he was inside the building.
He wished Amelia was beside him to hold his hand.

Once they'd found a place to sit, Mud had no idea what to
expect. He kept his eyes on Nick, Vi, and everyone else
around so he knew what to do. He stood when they stood,
sat when they sat, clapped when they clapped and closed his
eyes when they all prayed. The singing part was weird. Some
people had their hands in the air, including Nick and Vi, and
there were a couple of people who even kneeled down.
Mud's throat constricted as the music played. This grief was
so annoying. And he wasn't even thinking about Griff.

The problem was, the tightness in his throat continued
throughout the rest of the service, even when the preacher
kept talking for over half an hour. It was hard to concentrate
on his words when waves of emotion kept washing over him
like a warm breeze in summer or maybe like a cool drink. A
difficult sensation to describe. It was all he could do to not

weep again, but he didn't want to mess up Nick's church service so he sucked it all in again.

When they finally announced the close Nick turned to him, eyebrows raised. "So? What did you think?"

Mud shook his head. "So weird." He opened his mouth to explain when Vi grabbed Nick's arm and pointed to the back of the auditorium.

"Amelia's here, look."

Mud swiveled in sync with Nick to see where she pointed. It was true. Amelia stood near the exit and cast a sheepish smile back at them, lifting her hand in a little wave.

It was strange when they all waved back at the same time. Vi squeezed past Nick, obviously to go see her.

Mud turned back to Nick. "Doesn't she normally come?"

A small crease appeared between Nick's eyes. "She did for a few weeks late last year but not since then, as far as I am aware." He jerked his chin in their direction. "Shall we say hi?"

"Sure." Mug shrugged, a cover for the way his heart was romping around in his chest the second he'd laid eyes on Amelia. At least he didn't have to process the church service right this second. He released a long breath as he approached Amelia. She was gorgeous as usual in a flowing blue skirt and white-ish top.

"Hey," he greeted her after Nick said his hellos. He shoved his hands in his pockets.

"Hey, Mud." She seemed as awkward as he felt. Yep, they definitely needed to clear the air. Probably should do that now before he thought about it too much.

"Shall we find some morning tea in the foyer?" Vi glanced from one to the other in the group.

"Thanks, but I'm going to ..." Amelia pointed to the doors

and backed away. "I'm going to head off." It seemed she was in a hurry to avoid him, but he didn't want to let her escape.

Mud turned to Nick. "I'll be back. I need to update her about YODELL." Lame excuse but it would suffice.

"No probs, bro." Nick's arm circled Vi's waist, and they moved off to wherever the morning tea was. Mud hurried after Amelia and caught up outside the external doors. "Meels, wait up."

She jolted to a stop but turned slowly to face him. Reluctantly?

"I'll walk you to your car." He fell into step beside her as she continued, and he noticed the corner of her mouth tweak upward.

"Your chivalry is astounding." Dry words slipped from her deadpan face.

Ten steps later, he realized why.

"Here's my car." She pressed her keyring. "Thank you, sir, for your kind escort."

Far out. He needed a head slap right about now. "Hilarious." He narrowed his eyes at her. "Do me a favor and lock it again."

"Why?" She raised eyebrows at him.

"Can we walk?"

She eyed him for a moment and then nodded briefly, locking her car and dropping her keys in her purse. "Where to?"

"Let's go over to the lake." Mud really wanted to hold her hand but kept his hands in his pockets as they strolled across to the parkland that lined the shore.

"I'm assuming this means you're ready to talk?"

"Ready might be an over-statement, but yeah." Mud laughed self-consciously.

Amelia paused. "You don't have to. I can wait."

NEVER SAY YOU NEED ME

"No. It's fine." Mud pulled his hands out and shook them, trying to release tension. "Gotta rip the band-aid off at some point." He glanced sideways at her as they continued. "Been doing plenty of that lately."

"I'm sure that's been hard." Amelia pressed her lips into a thin line.

Mud saw a bench seat ahead. "Let's sit."

Looking out over the picturesque waters was calming. The perfect setting in which to reveal one's inner turmoil. Mud angled toward Amelia and told her all about Griff, the accident, his reaction and how it all led him to Trinity Lakes. And, amazingly, he managed it without breaking down. Perhaps all the talks with Nick had begun the healing process. But Mud realized he still had a long way to go.

"I couldn't talk about it and the longer I kept silent, the harder it got to say anything." He hoped she would understand this explanation. "I'm so sorry I shut you out. Especially after telling you how much I enjoy being around you."

Amelia's eyes dropped to her knees. "It was confusing, I have to admit." Her fingers twisted together in her lap. "But I understand and I am sorry you're going through this." She lifted her eyes to his. "Please remember you have a friend here. You *can* talk to me about it whenever you want."

Mud reached out and snagged one of her hands in his. "Problem is, Meels, I don't want to be friends with you."

CHAPTER TWELVE

Amelia's heart slammed in her chest. *What?* He didn't want to be friends? Wait. He said that while holding her hand and threading his fingers through hers. Her mouth went dry and she found it hard to get any words out. "Wh … what do you mean?"

His eyes grazed her face, like she'd seen before. "I mean, I want more." He broke the intensity of his gaze and turned to the scene before them, but kept hold of her hand. "I know I'm a mess and I know you have no reason to trust me, but I am working on it all, trying to change. And I don't want to wait until I get to the other side of all this." He let out a long breath, then finally turned back to her. "I'm hoping you feel the same. Can we try?"

Amelia swallowed hard. "Me?"

One side of Mud's mouth curved up, and he looked around the park. "I don't see anyone else here."

Her tongue seemed to stick to the roof of her mouth. Although her infatuation had rapidly morphed into a deeper attachment, this was still the guy who "loved 'em and left 'em". As much as she'd once admired such detachment, she now wanted far more. "I can't do the no-strings thing."

Mud leaned closer, his thumb caressing her hand. "That's what I mean about changing. I want some entanglement this time." He feathered a kiss on her cheek then whispered in her ear. "I can't get you out of my mind."

Thrills shot through her at his nearness and his words. She bit down on her lip as that familiar yearning for love rose to the surface. Maybe this was it. Or at least the start of it. Maybe she owed it to herself to take a leap. "Me either," she murmured.

It was as if he'd waited expectantly for some sign from her. The second the words were out, he captured her lips with his and the universe spun again, the same as last time. Amelia was in deep, deep trouble where her heart was concerned, but she had no desire to fight it.

She would have become lost in his kisses but he drew away after a moment, his eyes bright. "I wanna take you on a date."

"Like we've never been out together." She rolled her eyes.

"Not as an official 'couple,' we haven't." He lifted his index fingers as quotation marks.

Amelia's stomach flipped again. A couple. That would take a minute to get used to. "Sure. Where are you taking me?"

"How does a twilight picnic with a campfire sound?"

"It sounds dark and smoky." Amelia tried to keep her face straight.

Mud's shoulders slumped a little. "You don't want to?"

She couldn't hide her amusement as she frowned. "Of course I want to. I happen to like dark and smoky."

Mud narrowed his eyes and poked her in the ribs, making her squeal. "You are trouble, you know that, Meels?"

"More than you can possibly imagine," she said. "So, when is this date? I'll bring the smores."

"Friday night, I reckon."

After this revelation? He was going to make her wait five days? Mud must have read her thoughts because he slipped an arm around her waist and pulled her close.

"But we can have lots of mini dates between now and then."

He kissed her softly, once again sending her into a spiral.

True to his word, they caught up every day that week. Sometimes for a coffee, and sometimes for a long phone conversation—particularly on the days when he was low with grief again and he didn't want to be out and about. Amelia was happy to give him that space, especially since he was open about it now, and she figured he would be better again the next day.

Friday came around soon enough and Amelia looked forward to their date with more than a few butterflies taking up residence in her stomach. As yet, neither of them had told Nick or Vi that they were exploring a relationship. Amelia wasn't sure if Vi would approve, and Mud told her he didn't want Nick to get on his case.

"Why would Nick be on your case?" Amelia asked him as they drove to the campgrounds out of town on the lake.

Mud shrugged, keeping his eyes on the road. "My history, I guess. He'll want to make sure I treat you right."

"As a good friend should."

"True. I don't really have a satisfactory reason to keep it from him, do I?" He sighed. "But if I do share, that would mean Vi hears as well. Why don't you want her to know?"

"She'll want to protect me from you." Amelia's lips twitched.

"As a good friend should."

They both laughed. "Okay. So we should tell them, do you think?"

"Probably." Mud nodded. "We can do it together." He reached across and squeezed her hand.

They drove in comfortable silence for a few minutes until Mud uttered an oath and pulled the car over seconds after entering the campgrounds.

"What's wrong?" Alarm shot through Amelia.

"Idiots." Mud got out of the car and slammed the door. Amelia heard the trunk open and some thumping noises before it closed again. With shivers coiling up her spine, she climbed out of the car in time to see him toss a thick blanket onto his shoulder, hoist a large water carrier and jog over to a group of teens. But then she froze, her brain non-compliant in the face of Mud's sudden change and the huge fire before her.

"What are you doing?" Mud yelled as he emptied the water onto their bonfire.

"Hey, who do you think you are?" One teen with an attitude tried to shove him away.

Mud barely shifted his footing and kept working on the blaze. "Someone who's seen how fires like this become raging forest infernos."

A couple of other youths laughed and mocked. "Look who's a big chicken." One of them picked up a spray can, ready to aim at the flames.

"Don't you dare." Mud's tone was almost dangerous. "Put it down right now. What, do you have a death wish?"

The teen must have seen sense, or at least the wild look in Mud's eyes, as he dropped the can. Amelia watched from a distance, her arms limp by her side, unsure of what to do, as Mud beat down any remaining flames with the blanket.

Mud put all his energy into dousing the fire, anger radiating from his whole being. "Look, I'm a firefighter." He finally turned to explain. "This is reckless. You're within two meters of this pine tree and any flying sparks could easily ignite it. You haven't even cleared the area of dried leaves and pine needles. Don't even get me started on spraying flammable liquid. This is a recipe for disaster. If you're going to have a fire, do it safely."

Mud tossed the ruined blanket aside, picked up the empty carrier and stalked back to the car. Amelia quietly climbed in beside him, still shocked by what she'd witnessed. She was about to ask him what it was all about when she realized he was trembling and breathing hard.

"Are you alright?"

His hands tightened and loosened on the steering wheel and she saw sweat trickle down the side of his face. "I will be in a minute." He closed his eyes and she saw his lips moving. Was he praying? Or perhaps counting?

She sat in silence, wondering what was going on, until finally he spoke again. "I should probably tell you about the PTSD."

Amelia thought for a moment. "Post-traumatic stress disorder?" She studied the deep lines on his forehead. "I'm guessing this isn't about your brother?"

"No." He made a sound that might have been a choked sob. "That just added to the load." He blew out a long breath and started the engine. "Let's get our nice, contained, safe campfire set up and I'll tell you the whole story."

Did this have something to do with fire? "We can skip the fire if you're not up to it."

He looked across at her and squeezed her hand. "It's fine. I want to do it. And sorry if I scared you before."

Amelia nodded. It would have been less scary if she'd

understood it. But he'd promised to tell her so she hoped it would be fine.

They drove to a large clearing and found a previously dug fire pit. Mud scraped the area clear of leaves with a shovel, re-filled his water carrier at the lake's edge, then collected firewood from the trunk and carefully built a small, cozy campfire. "Umm, sorry I wrecked the picnic blanket." He raked a hand through his hair.

"Never mind. We still have these." Amelia withdrew a couple of cushions from the trunk and tossed them on the ground nearby—but not too close. Soon they sat beside the warm blaze as the sun dipped below the horizon and the air cooled.

"There was a massive bush fire in Australia last summer." Mud began his story with no warning and Amelia snapped to attention.

"I volunteered to help fight it. People are really harsh on firefighters, complaining when their properties or animals aren't saved, but they have no idea." Mud swallowed hard. "Same as what your firies suffered in LA this year.

"The fires in Australia were driven by fierce winds, gusts up to a hundred kilometers—sorry, sixty odd miles per hour —so you can imagine how fast the fire moved. Flames one hundred feet tall that jumped twenty miles ahead and stole the oxygen from the air. And we were trying to drive firetrucks down rutted dirt tracks with minimum visibility, trying to keep ahead of the inferno."

"That's …" There were no words for the horror she felt at his description. Amelia reached out and put a hand on his knee instead and his hand soon wrapped around hers.

"There was this house out in the bush. The family refused to leave wanting to defend their property. When we got there the fire was already on the perimeter. We found the husband unconscious on the ground near the gate—like I said, the oxygen was gone. We weren't aware of the wife and kids until we heard their screams." Mud swallowed, then swallowed again, his voice choked. "We couldn't get to them in time. The heat claimed them before we even entered the house. I saw ..." Mud groaned and gripped her hand even tighter. So tight, she winced in pain. "I saw them burn, Amelia. Only a glimpse before we had to run. But there is no way I will ever forget that sight."

———

MUD REALIZED how tight he gripped Amelia's hand and let it go abruptly, wiping the moisture from his cheeks. "Sorry." He focused on his breathing. He didn't want to freak out a second time in one evening. Didn't want to put Amelia through that.

"I still have nightmares. I have panic attacks sometimes. And that's why I stopped those kids tonight."

Amelia's eyes were wide and full of sympathy. "And that's why you brought that huge water carrier along."

He nodded, lips pressed together.

She scooted closer and wrapped her arms around him. "Thanks for telling me."

Mud buried his face in the soft curve of her neck, his arms around her waist. He breathed deeply, drinking in her comforting scent. "You have one up on Nick now."

Amelia drew back. "You haven't told him?"

Mud rubbed his face. "Nah. I'm not good at this stuff. Pretty lousy really."

Amelia rubbed circles on his back but said nothing.

"I guess ... it's like ... with Dad always happy-go-lucky, I thought that was normal, you know? That's how I was supposed to be. Now I'm learning it's *not* normal, that his brain injury made him like that." He shrugged, a little confused by his own revelations. "But when you're a kid you see your dad as the standard, the model to live by. Does that make sense?"

"One hundred percent." Amelia's words were emphatic, but she had shifted her gaze to the last colors of the sunset.

Mud sat up straight. That was enough emotion for now. "Time for food, yeah?"

She looked back at him with a small smile. "What've you got?"

"I'm gonna chuck some spuds in the coals, and while they're cooking, I'll fry up some steak. How does that sound?"

"Sounds great. But what are spuds?"

Mud chuckled. "The good old potato. Nothing fancy."

"Right." Amelia's smile reflected his. "Can I help?"

Mud collected potatoes and foil and asked Amelia to wrap them while he made a space for them among the glowing coals. Once the potatoes were in the fire he pulled out a cast iron pan which he nestled on the burning wood.

"Where'd you get all this stuff?" Amelia asked.

Mud grinned. "Nick's an excellent resource."

"Of course." She was quiet for a moment, watching him work. "Can I ask you something?"

"Sure."

She was aware of his darkest secrets now. He had nothing to hide. "What made you go to church last week?"

Mud paused for a minute and rocked back on his heels. "I have a lot of questions," he said. "Mostly about life and death. Trying to find answers." He turned his attention back to the pan, seasoning the steak.

"And?" Amelia pressed. "Are you finding any?"

He shrugged. "Maybe." He would probably need to go again, since grief or something had plagued and distracted him the whole service. "How about you?"

"Same." Her lips stretched into a thin line again. "Questions."

"Will you be there this Sunday?"

"Probably."

"Wanna go together?"

"That would mean telling our besties beforehand." She smiled at him.

Mud put his tongs down. "Are you ready for that?"

She looked down and picked at her fingernails. "I'm not sure. I mean, how serious is this?" Her eyes rose to his. "Aren't you going back to Australia after the wedding?"

Mud's stomach sank. He hadn't even thought about that. He'd been so caught up in his grief over Griff and his attraction to Amelia, he hadn't really thought long term. Sure, Amelia was more than a fleeting romance. Much more. Yet, he hadn't considered the fact they were from different countries, and how that might work practically.

He returned to the fire, frowning over the pan as he flipped the steaks. How to answer her? He drew in a deep breath and turned to her again. Honesty was the best choice, right? "Look, I don't want to be flippant and make promises I can't keep. I'm not sure what the future holds. But I do know I want this." He waved a hand back and forth between them. "I want to explore if there is a future between us."

Amelia's gaze drifted to her fingers. "Okay. So we tell them we are simply seeing each other and don't make it sound too serious." She let out a little huff.

Mud lifted the pan from the fire with a thick mitt, then crawled over to her. He cupped her face with one hand. "Look at me, Meels."

She hesitated and blinked before her eyes met his.

"I *am* serious about you. More serious than I've ever been about anyone. Like, I can't get enough of you. You're so amazing, so beautiful." He shifted back from her, his heart throbbing in a way he hadn't experienced before. Almost aching. "But this is all new to me, this kind of depth. It's gonna take time to adjust."

Amelia's eyes seemed to be fixed on his lips. "Right. We're keeping it light for their sake," she murmured.

"Mm-hmm." He brushed a thumb over her cheek and released her. "Ready for some grub?" The intimacy growing between them was overwhelming and he needed to break the moment.

A small frown creased her brow, and she shook her head as though clearing fog. "Grub?"

"Food."

Amelia sat up straighter and cleared her throat. "As long as you're not cooking actual grubs over there, I'm happy to eat."

"As if."

"Well, I've heard about you Aussies. What are they called? Watchy … wenchy … witchery grubs?"

Mud laughed. "You mean witchetty grubs? I've never tried them. Although I've heard they taste like chicken."

Amelia screwed up her nose in that way that made her look adorable. "Well, it all sounds like witchcraft to me." She put on a sinister voice and waved her hands as if over a cauldron. "Add the guts of six witchetty grubs and six alligator teeth."

"Yeah, nah." Mud laughed as he scooped potatoes out of the fire. "It would have to be croc teeth. We don't have alligators."

Amelia rolled her eyes. "Whatever. And just so you know, everyone says weird food tastes like chicken."

"Well, I don't have any chicken or weird food tonight. Nothing but pure beef."

"Thank goodness for that." Amelia over-dramatized the words.

They enjoyed their meal in silence, except for expressions of pleasure at the taste. It seemed she thought he was a wonderful cook. Campfire food might be the extent of his talent there, but he enjoyed her appreciation of his endeavors.

When she'd finished and wiped grease from her fingers with a napkin, she opened the tote bag she'd brought. "My turn." She looked at him. "Can you find me a stick to roast the marshmallows?"

Mud put his plate down. "On it." He returned two minutes later with a suitable twig.

"Thank you." She smiled sweetly at him, making his insides turn over.

Amelia put what he would have called biscuits, but she called crackers on a plate, and topped them with pieces of chocolate. Then she set about toasting a marshmallow over the hot coals. Next she put the melting marshmallow onto the chocolate and covered it with another cracker, making a sandwich, and handed it to him. "This is a s'more."

Mud took a bite. The combination of crunch, chocolaty goodness and gooey marshmallow was delicious. "So good." He said around the treat in his mouth.

"Right?"

They ate several more until Mud cried mercy, at which she giggled, a sound that reminded him of crystal chimes. "Hey, come here." He waved her over and she shifted closer. "You've got chocolate on your chin."

"Oh." She reached for a napkin.

"I've got it." He wiped the smudge from her chin with his thumb, then kissed the spot where the chocolate had been. "You'd better check if I've got any," he murmured.

Amelia's eyes scanned his face, and her lips twitched. "Oh, you have it everywhere." She kissed his chin, his cheeks, his nose and finally landed on his mouth. He swore every nerve in his entire body came to life as their kisses deepened. But when he moved to lie back on the cushions, she pulled away from him and created some distance. Mud clenched his teeth. *Stupid.* He was moving too fast for her.

One thing he knew, dating this stunning woman was fast becoming the best time of his life.

CHAPTER THIRTEEN

Sunday came around all too quickly and Amelia's stomach churned at the thought of telling Violet her news. She and Mud had agreed they'd each tell their best friend separately before church, at approximately the same time. They didn't want Nick to tell Violet or vice versa. Although it would be easier for Mud since he stayed in Nick's house.

Amelia glanced at her smart watch. He was probably doing it right now, while Amelia waited outside Vi's place. Honestly, she didn't need to wait. She had a key and Vi had given her permission to come and go as she pleased, but Amelia's jitters held her back. What would Vi say? It didn't matter that Amelia had imagined a thousand different ways to tell her, she still hadn't landed on an option that stopped the butterflies swarming in her stomach. Why Violet's approval meant so much, she couldn't say.

Finally Violet opened the door, and seeing Amelia, lifted her brows. "Oh, hey. What are you doing here?"

"Um ... I thought I might come with you this morning. To

church, that is." Amelia internally scolded herself for the way she stammered.

"Of course you can." Violet immediately gave her a hug.

Once they were on the road Amelia drew in a deep breath and let it out slowly. Now was her chance. "I wanted to tell you something."

"Sure. What's that?"

"Well ... I'm ... I'm seeing someone." Amelia watched Vi's face for her reaction.

To her surprise, Violet's face lit up with a wide grin. "I knew it. It's Mud, isn't it?"

"Uh ... yeah." Amelia wondered how Vi had figured it out.

"Nick and I were just saying the other day, 'imagine if our best friends got together.'"

Vi looked at her sideways and must have seen a look of disbelief on her face. "What? We compared notes and realized you were both 'unavailable' at the same times for the last week."

Heat rose in Amelia's cheeks. Had it been that easy to work out? "Well, it's early days. We're just testing the waters, so to speak."

Vi's face became serious. "Keep your eyes wide open, Amelia. Mud is ... well ... Mud."

"I'm well aware," Amelia answered. But Mud seemed to be changing, unless it was all fake. Oh, but the way he'd looked at her when he told her he couldn't get enough of her —she'd bought it hook, line and possibly the whole infernal rod. The heat in her cheeks flared higher. "I'm being careful." Although it was hard not to race into something headlong when she wanted it so much.

Vi glanced briefly at her again. "Have you spoken to Bree?"

Goodness. Bree. Amelia hadn't even thought about that.

"Umm ... no." Her voice came out like a squeak, but she lifted a shoulder, trying to sound casual. "I'm sure she'll be fine. She's got a new man and everything now."

"But it would be a courtesy to tell her, at least. I mean, you'll be seeing her plenty as the wedding gets closer."

Amelia let her gaze fall to her lap and twisted her fingers together. "Yeah, I know. Okay, I'll go see her."

"Good girl." Vi smiled. "Now, tell me. Mud? How did this happen?"

Amelia rolled her eyes. "Do you mean to tell me you never picked up on the massive crush I had on him last year?"

"No." Violet's mouth gaped. "Wait. Oh, I remember you being weird a couple of times. Is that what was going on?"

Amelia sighed. "Yeah. But he barely knew I existed. Flamboyant Bree got all his attention." Why did that thought still sting a little?

"And now?"

"Well, we started getting to know each other after the hit-and-run. You wouldn't believe it, but we have heaps in common. So, I guess one thing led to another, and here we are."

"Naw." Vi squeezed her hand. "So Mud has discovered how amazing my best friend is, has he? It's about time someone noticed. And you really like him?"

"I really do." Amelia's breath left her as she admitted it.

"I hope it works out for you both. I mean that."

"Me too."

"Hey, we could go on a double date." Vi's tone was enthusiastic as she pulled into the church parking lot. "What do you think?"

Amelia's heart did a little flip. "That would be cool. We can ask Mud and Nick."

Vi opened her mouth to say something, but Amelia cut her off. "He's told Nick about us this morning, too."

Vi laughed. "Well planned."

Inside the church, Nick and Mud already sat in the pew about halfway toward the front. Mud gave her a slight nod and wink as she approached. Violet moved to sit with Nick, leaving Amelia room to sit next to Mud, who immediately took her hand. He leaned in and whispered in her ear. "How did you go?"

"All good." She was still a little breathless. It seemed surreal, like perhaps she imagined it all. "You?"

"Seems they'd already guessed, hey."

"Mm-hmm." Amelia nodded. "Vi wants to go on a double date."

A slow smile spread across Mud's face. "Let's do it. I'll sort out the details with Nick."

The singing started and they stood up together. Mud kept hold of her hand throughout most of the service, which didn't help her focus on the preaching at all. She was far too aware of his nearness and spent most of the time wondering what he was thinking. Was he listening to the message, or did his mind drift like hers?

When the service finished, they headed to the foyer to enjoy morning tea.

"Did Nick give you the third degree as you expected?" Amelia asked Mud as they stood to the side, waiting for their friends to join them.

"And the fifth and the eight hundredth." Mud rolled his eyes. "Did Vi warn you away from me?"

Amelia's lips twitched. "Big, bad, monster were the words she used, I think."

"Serious?" Mud's brows lifted almost to his hairline.

Amelia laughed out loud, and Mud shook his head.

"You'll keep."

"Sorry. Not sorry." Amelia tried to hide her amusement. "No, she was actually supportive. Cautiously supportive."

"So you got off easy?" Mud's eyes narrowed, although his lips curved upward.

"Not so much." Amelia stared into her coffee cup. "I have to go see Bree."

"Why?"

"She *is* one of my best friends, you know." She raised her gaze to his. "It's the right thing to do."

Mud looked uncomfortable and sipped his drink, shoving his free hand into his pocket. "Sure. I guess so. Do you want me to come with you?"

Amelia put out her hand and rested it on his forearm. "It's fine. It will be better if I go on my own."

"Okay." Mud's gaze drifted away from her and she sensed his disquiet.

"Do you not want me to go on my own?"

Mud shrugged and swallowed.

Amelia's stomach went cold. "On Friday night, you said—"

"I said I want us to be together." Mud rounded on her, put his cup on a nearby table and took her hands in his. "And that hasn't changed. It's just..." His eyes darted around the room, back to her again and then down at their clasped hands. "Bree will have nothing nice to say about me."

Amelia tried to stop her lips from tweaking. "Is that what's bothering you? You suspect she might turn me against you?"

"Umm. Yeah." The words came out slowly, and he finally raised his eyes to hers again.

Amelia squeezed his hands. "I've already heard it all. Best friends, remember?"

"And you still want to be with me?"

She sighed. "To be honest, there was a lot of weighing the pros and cons but like you, I'm ready to take a chance."

A lop-sided grin developed on his face. "I'd love to hear what the pros are."

There was no way she would bare her soul surrounded by other people, so she opted for something lighthearted. "Let's see." She held her fingers up as if to count. "He can put out a fire. He's not bad as a chauffeur—"

"Alright. Alright." Mud rolled his eyes. "Let's go for lunch somewhere?"

Amelia pressed her lips together. "Sorry. I already texted Bree and she's agreed to catch up this afternoon. I'll call you tonight, okay?"

———

DESPITE AMELIA'S REASSURANCES, Mud was antsy all afternoon and evening until she called.

"So, how'd it go?" he asked as soon as he picked up the phone.

"Well, she knows now, so that's a plus." Amelia's voice sounded a little flat.

"But?" Mud tried to draw her out.

"Let's just say there might be some tension between us for a while." Her sigh was audible.

"She wasn't happy, I take it?" Mud's shoulders sagged. The last thing he wanted was to cause problems in a long-standing friendship, but this was all his fault. If he'd never messed around with Bree's feelings in the first place, there wouldn't be this strain now. "I'm really sorry, Meels."

She was quiet for a moment. "It's okay. She'll get over it."

"But what about you? Are you alright?" Whatever had

happened must have hurt, and Mud's throat thickened real-izing it was his responsibility.

"I'll be fine. It will all be fine." Amelia's words were forced.

Mud ran a hand through his hair. "I wish I was there with you right now."

Silence again for a beat. "Me too."

"I can come over." Mud was ready to jump in the car at the slightest hint.

"No. It's all good. I need some sleep." The words sounded rushed. "I'll see you tomorrow, I guess."

"Okay. Tomorrow."

They spoke for a few more minutes and then rang off, but guilt still weighed on him. The more he thought about all Nick had said over the years, added to what he now heard in church, the more he became convinced of his need to change. And not minor change either. He needed a life-alter-ing, fundamental change. A whole new path.

At the auto shop the next morning he broached the topic with Brandon as they worked together on a Chevy truck. "Hey Mac." Because he was an Aussie who nicknamed every person he spent time with, and Brand-o didn't roll off the tongue well, shortening McAffrey to Mac was perfect. "You go to church and everything, yeah?"

Brandon's mouth curved in a lopsided grin, although he kept his focus on what he was doing. "You know it."

"Can I ask you a question?" Nerves fluttered in Mud's gut though he couldn't figure out why.

This time Brandon put down his tools. "Sounds like it's time for a break. Coffee?" He raised his eyebrows as he wiped the grease from his hands.

"Sure. Okay." Mud followed Brandon to the break room, wondering why the man had dismissed him so casually.

Brandon poured two coffees and motioned for Mud to sit. As soon as he did, Brandon took the chair opposite and looked at him straight. "What's your question?"

The tips of Mud's ears burned, and he shifted in his seat. "It wasn't that important. Gee." Except it was, and it churned within him.

"Well, we're here now. Shoot." Brandon eased the tension a little with a shrug.

Mud fiddled with the mug, turning it this way and that, watching the steam float around the rim. "I've been to church a couple of times lately. With Nick, you know." He glanced up briefly to see if Brandon was listening. He was. "It's weird. I keep getting emotional when I'm there. At first I thought it was only grief over my brother, but now I keep seeing what a mess I've made of everything. Like, my whole life is playing out before me—every bad decision, selfish act, harsh word—and I'm kind of disgusted with myself. I don't know what's wrong with me. Six months ago I couldn't have cared less."

"Sounds like Jesus is chasing you down, bro." Brandon grinned at him.

"What do you mean?" And why was it so amusing? "I'm not sure I even believe in God."

"Just because you don't believe in something doesn't mean it doesn't exist," Brandon sipped his coffee. "What you're experiencing, we might call conviction."

"Conviction?"

"It's when you see your sin through God's eyes," Brandon explained. "It makes you want to change, right?"

"Um … well … yeah." Exactly. "But it doesn't feel good. I thought this Christian stuff was all about peace and joy."

And there was that half smile again. "Oh, it is, but it's also about being transformed, and transformation is not painless

in my experience. But it is one hundred percent worth it."
Brandon drained his cup, looking thoughtful. "Can I tell you
what the Bible says?"

Mud shrugged. "Sure. Nick already told me to read it, but
I haven't read much yet."

"Nick is a wise man." Brandon's lips twitched again. "In a
book called Romans, it says that while we were still sinners,
Christ died for us. It doesn't matter how bad your past looks,
His sacrifice covered it all. In another part of the Bible it says
if we confess our sins, He is faithful and just and will forgive
us and purify us."

Brandon's words triggered some kind of deep yearning
and Mud's eyes burned. But he didn't want to get emotional
at work in a garage of all places. He gulped down the last of
his coffee and shoved the chair away from the table. "Yeah,
thanks for that Mac. I appreciate it."

"Do yourself a favor. Keep reading what Nick told you
to." Brandon also rose and took the mugs to the sink. It
seemed he took the hint that Mud had had enough for today.
"Hey, I've been meaning to ask, how's the search going for
the hit-and-run driver?"

"Not great." Mud was thankful for the change of subject,
though he would process Brandon's words later. "We're sure
it's the right car but don't know how to prove it, or that he
was the one driving. All we've learned is that this guy is a
tutor and operates from home."

"A tutor, hey?" Brandon's brows drew together. "I have a
couple of friends in the education system. Maybe they've
heard of him. Give me his details and I'll ask around."

"Sure." Mud nodded. "Any help at this stage is
appreciated."

Mud didn't hear anything back from him for the rest of
the week, though, and between the troubled thoughts that

continued to plague him, his only respite came from moments with his new girlfriend.

Girlfriend. Yeah, that's how he saw her now. The one light that shone in his world of darkness. Nick and Brandon seemed to think God would bring light to his life. As he read the Bible it said much the same. That Jesus was the light that overcame darkness. But that sounded so airy fairy—so out of reach.

Amelia was real, tangible, and here. Holding and kissing her gave him some comfort. Respite from the grief and nightmares. Her wit made him laugh and provoked inane conversations. Meaningless silliness. Relief from his more serious, dark thoughts. Her presence centered him and was a steadying influence that gave respite from the sense of having the rug pulled from beneath him.

They often met at the gym, or for coffee, but always the light in her eyes gave him hope and energy. And it was no different when they visited the vintage cinema with Nick and Vi the following Saturday. Foo was running the original *Rocky* film for the week and the four of them were keen to see it on the big screen.

"Hey, gorgeous," Mud whispered in Amelia's ear as the credits started rolling. "Do you wanna go horse riding tomorrow?"

"Aren't you going to church this time?" She turned toward him.

"Well, I suppose." Perhaps he wanted to avoid the uncomfortable sensations it brought for once. "Are you?"

"I suppose." She grinned as she mimicked his response.

Mud smirked at her. "We can go riding after church I guess."

"I would love that." Amelia offered him a genuine smile and stood up to follow Nick and Vi out of the cinema.

"This is a great place," Vi said as they entered the foyer. "Why have I never been here before?"

"Yeah, I love it." Amelia walked next to her.

"Nick," Mud chimed in. "You should bring Vi here more often."

Nick laughed self-consciously, then gazed around. "True. Linyu Foo has done a great job with renovating."

"He has, hasn't he?" Amelia grinned.

Nick nodded. "I've done some electrical work here."

"Oho, you need some approval, mate?" Mud laughed.

Nick's face reddened. "No. That's not what I meant. The whole building has been rewired to current standards."

"Yes." Amelia's smile widened. "Foo would have complied with all the building codes when he renovated."

Nick shrugged. "Exactly. Just as he should."

Mud slid an arm around Amelia's waste. "Another reason to keep coming back, hey Meels?" He winked at her. As if he needed an excuse.

CHAPTER FOURTEEN

Amelia's heart warmed at the encouragement they all had for her friend. Hopefully, with all the positive feedback, Foo's cinema would become more profitable. She knew from previous visits and conversations that it had been a struggle at first. But hopefully this retro movie idea was growing in popularity. Certainly, gauging the response of her friends, they had enjoyed the experience.

When the others headed to the parking lot, Amelia headed to the counter. "Hi Foo." She waved and waited for him to finish with a customer.

"Hey, Amelia. What's up?" He greeted her after the patron walked away.

"My friend Nick, who was here with us tonight, said he's done some electrical work for you. He was very complimentary. Actually, they all were. You're doing a great job here."

Foo's face broke into a wide smile. "Thank you so much. It's good to hear the encouragement. Nick's a great guy. He's the first one I call now when I need electrical work done."

Yeah, Nick was great, but not as great as his buff best

friend. Amelia bit her lip at the thought of Mud, who seemed to never be far from her mind. "Well, it's good to know you're doing well."

"Thanks, Amelia. I appreciate your encouragement." Foo nodded and Amelia headed for the doors.

The next morning she got ready for church, deciding on jeans and a nice blouse since she would be horse-riding later in the day. She put a hat, t-shirt and boots in a bag, ready to change after church. Part of her had hoped Mud would say he didn't want to go to church, and then she would have refused as well.

Amelia still hadn't talked with Violet about the other week. About the craving for belonging, for family, for love. Was this intense connection she had with Mud love? Certainly she had experienced nothing like it with Cody. Though she'd thought that was love at the time. Until she became Cody's caddy. She smirked at the term she'd coined for her ex.

No. With Mud it was different. Sometimes the way he looked at her was overwhelming. Like she was his entire universe. An amazing sensation but also terrifying. What would happen when the newness wore off and became the everyday? Would he still see her the same way? Despite his assurances, she wasn't sure if he'd stick around.

As she sat in the church beside him, she sensed tension in his arm as he clasped her hand. She tried not to worry about what it meant and to focus on the sermon, which was hard, until the preacher mentioned a particular verse in the Bible.

"For I have loved you with an everlasting love."

If Amelia had been a puppy, everyone around her would have seen her ears prick up. Her heart fluttered immediately at those words. What was he saying?

"The Lord knew each of you before you were born, and

has had His hand upon you, set you apart, chosen you. Know that He has always been and always will work for your best."

Amelia realized her palm became moist and pulled her hand from Mud's grasp to wipe it on her jeans.

"And there is nothing you can do, or have done in the past, that will change his mind. In Romans, it says 'For I am convinced that neither death nor life, neither angels nor demons, neither the present nor the future, nor any powers, neither height nor depth, nor anything else in all creation, will be able to separate us from the love of Christ Jesus our Lord.'"

Amelia became aware her mouth was hanging open and quickly closed it, swallowing. This kind of love sounded fierce, protective, unwavering. Everything she wanted. She really needed to have a talk with Vi to sort out these crazy thoughts.

Later, when she sat astride a gentle mare, with Mud riding beside her, she asked him what he thought about the service.

Mud let out a harsh laugh. "Apart from the tightness in my throat and chest, I guess it was alright."

"Tightness?" Did he have some kind of episode? Seizure?

"Nah, it's nothing." He shrugged. "Probably the PTSD playing up. What did you think?"

"I liked what the preacher said," she mumbled, unsure of his reception.

"Yeah, me too."

"It's kind of out there though, isn't it?"

"A hundred percent." Mud nodded, eyes wide. "I'm wondering if I keep going there, am I gonna end up like one of those weirdo happy-clappies?"

Amelia couldn't hide her laugh. "I can't imagine it."

Mud's lips thinned into a line. "Would it be a problem for you if I did?" He glanced sideways at her.

"Is that a serious question?" She couldn't bring herself to admit her thoughts leaned the same way.

"Nah." The corner of his mouth turned up and he turned his attention to the horse's head, stroking its neck. "I'm just messing. Wanna give these animals a run?"

Amelia nudged her mare into a canter. "Thought you'd never ask," she called as she sped away from him, laughing.

She reined in on a rise that overlooked the three lakes that basked in the sunshine. Mud soon pulled up beside her.

"There's nothing like magnificent scenery, is there?" He gazed out over the vista.

Amelia turned to him and tried to keep her face straight. "You're a big softie under all that fun and bluster, aren't you?"

"What are you saying?" His eyebrow cocked in mock offence. "There's nothing unmanly about admiring nature." He slid from the saddle and tethered his horse to a tree.

Amelia copied him and strode over to where he stood, taking in the landscape below, with hazy mountains in the distance. He turned to her and slipped his arms around her waist. "I particularly like admiring this view." He dropped a kiss on her lips and warmth spread through her.

"Well, you're not too hard on the eyes, either," she murmured just in time before he kissed her again.

A few breathless minutes later they pulled apart, then sat together on a rock where they could enjoy the scenery. Amelia rested her head on his shoulder. "Can I ask you something?"

"Mm-hmm."

"Have you thought any more about what you'll do after the wedding?" Because, heaven help her, she was becoming far too attached to this man. What if he upped and left to go back to Australia? She didn't want to consider what that separation might do to her. At the same time, she wanted to know. Needed to know. Was there any way to protect her heart?

"Sorry, Meels." He planted a kiss on the top of her head. "There's been too much going on inside my mind to think that far ahead." He was quiet for a moment, then continued. "I have some pretty big decisions to make, but I don't want to make any promises I can't keep. All I know is that things have to change."

Amelia lifted her head to look at him, panic rising. "Change?"

"Not between us." He brushed a hand down her cheek and gently kissed her again. "No. This is the *only* thing I'm sure about right now."

Amelia searched his eyes, still anxious. "What if the changes you need to make do affect us?" She had no idea what he referred to but if they were as big as he implied, everything could change. Couldn't it?

Mud cupped her face in his hands, caressing her cheeks. "That is the last thing I want." He paused and shifted his gaze to the lakes for a moment, then locked eyes with her again. "If I'm being honest, I'm not sure what the future holds." He drew her in tight and held her, stroking her hair. "All I know is—"

Mud's phone rang breaking into their moment. He drew back and pulled it from his pocket, checking the screen. "It's Mac ... Brandon." He stood up and walked a few paces away. "Hey Mac."

Amelia watched his face as he talked, unable to make out the other side of the conversation.

"Yeah? Is that right?"

He rubbed the back of his neck as he listened and nodded.

"That's good to know. Thanks. I'll look into it."

He ended the call and walked back to her, his eyes bright. "It seems one of Andy O'Dell's clients also happens to be his girlfriend."

———

SAVED BY THE BELL? Perhaps.

Mud had been about to blurt words that might be premature. Especially given he'd just told Amelia he couldn't make her any promises about the future. So it would be a bad idea to tell her he thought he was falling in love with her. Right?

But now they were on another train of thought with this news about YODELL.

"How does that help?" Amelia's brow furrowed.

Mud shrugged. "Maybe it doesn't. But think about it. What if ... what if his girlfriend was the driver and he's protecting her for some reason?"

Amelia's eyes widened. "Oh, my goodness. That makes complete sense."

Mud winked at her and contrived a French accent while tapping his temple. "Zee leetle gray cells 'ave been working." He took her hand and led her back to the horses.

"Oh, monsieur." She batted her eyelashes at him. "But how can we prove it?"

"No idea." He reverted to his normal accent with a roll of his eyes.

Mud bent slightly to give her a leg up onto her mare. Once she was in the saddle, he mounted his horse and they headed back down the trail in silence. He assumed she wondered the same as him—how to find out more about O'Dell's girlfriend.

Sure enough, a few minutes later she started talking about it. "Who told you he had a girlfriend? Do they know her name? Perhaps we can find out more about her."

"Like trawling through her socials and stuff?" Mud nodded. "Yeah, good idea. I'll see what I can find out." That would be a first step, anyhow.

"Do you think we'll ever see a resolution for the boy and his dog? I mean, who is going to pay for all the boy's medical expenses?" Amelia sounded wistful.

"It's hard to know." Mud guided his horse into the yards back at the ranch. "Look at it this way. At least we can be sure we've done our best to help."

"Yes, I suppose." She didn't sound convinced, though, and her brow remained creased as he dismounted.

"Well now, miss." Mud put on a Texan drawl. "Let me help you down from that fearsome steed."

At last she smiled at him, and seemed happy to slide from the saddle into his arms. "Why, thank you, sir." She rewarded him with a kiss on the cheek.

When she left him that evening, he felt bereft. How was it he missed her after five minutes? Man, he had it bad. Really bad. Or was it good? A bit of both?

Mud needed to make decisions. Needed to take steps forward so he might have a better idea of the future. If he found some stability, he'd make better decisions about Amelia and where their relationship was headed.

At the top of the list, he needed to call his mum. As if he was likely to forget. Nick asked him practically every day. But every day when he considered it, nausea threatened to take hold. He worried about how she'd respond, feared the brokenness in her voice, dreaded having everything dredged up once again. At some point he had to face it, and the longer he left it, the harder it got.

Even knowing that, it still took him several more days before he summoned the courage to make the call. The fact he had to wait until nearly midnight to get her at a good time made it even more nerve racking. He sat with Manny playing video games until Nick's flat mate headed to bed. There was still had an hour to kill waiting.

As he was about to dial, his heart ratcheted, and his breath came quickly. He recognized it—fight or flight as every muscle tensed. Oh yeah, flight would be so preferable right now, but he forced himself to concentrate on slowing his breathing. He pressed the call button.

"Mud? Is that you?"

Mud let out a long breath. She sounded more relieved than angry. Even so, Mud's eyes started burning and his throat constricted. "I'm sorry, Mum." The words sounded choked even to his own ears.

"Where are you? I've been so worried about you."

Mud squeezed his eyes shut, swiping at his cheeks. Another thing he never considered—making Mum's pain worse. "I'm still in the US. With Nick."

"You might have told us." Now that she'd got past the worry, the tension rose in her voice.

"I know, Mum. I've been really selfish, and I'm so sorry."

"You didn't even come to the funeral." Her voice broke, the hurt painfully clear.

"I know. I know." They were both crying now, their sobs mingling over the line.

"Why, Mud?"

"I don't know," he croaked. "I ... I couldn't face it."

Mum's voice softened, although she still sniffled. "You lost your brother."

"Yeah." The tears continued to flow. "I miss him."

"We all do, hon."

Mud scrambled for a tissue and blew his nose. "How is Dad?"

Mum sighed. "The same as ever."

He swallowed. Dad never had the capacity for a broad range of emotion after his accident. Always happy and joking. Which probably made it hard for Mum to grieve.

"Are you going to come home soon?" The tone of her voice told him how much she wished his answer would be today or tomorrow.

"Mum, I … I'm a mess." He pinched his nose. "I need to sort myself out."

"Can't you do that at home?" Obvious question.

"Nick is really helping me." *And Amelia.*

"Of course." The disappointment in her voice was palpable. "I understand. You two have always had a close bond. How long do you need?"

"Not sure, Mum. I don't want to make promises I can't keep." Pretty much the same as he'd said to Amelia.

They talked for a few more minutes before they ended the call and Mud sat on his bed, head in hands. Mum hadn't been as bad as he'd expected. And it made him think— maybe it was his own brokenness he feared. He remembered recent talks with Nick and how hard it'd been to express his feelings. Heck, he even avoided telling Amelia most of it. He'd deflected, downplayed, or rationalized every time their discussion deepened. And he'd shut down the conversation with Brandon the second he'd become vulnerable.

Mud rubbed his face. He'd thought he'd started to change, that he was getting better, but man, he still had a long way to go. It seemed like an insurmountable hurdle, a mountain range he couldn't cross. Brandon had said transformation was painful, but this? It was too much.

Truth was, he didn't want to bare his soul. But as he continued to work at the garage over the next few days, he realized a door had opened with Griff's death, and it was a door he was unable to shut. It was as if he was trying to hold back a tidal wave. Maybe it would drown him. Maybe it would drown those around him. No, he had to keep the walls in place. Stop them up with whatever he could find.

He worked the gym hard. He gamed with Nick, Manny or online until the early hours. And he often found solace in Amelia's company.

In trepidation, he joined her at church again on Sunday. Once again everything within him tensed, churned, upended. Stretched like a man on the rack, it was torture and he didn't know how to get any relief.

Near the end of the service Nick turned to him. "Have you thought about opening your heart to Jesus?"

Mud shook his head. Opening his heart to anyone right now would be the end of him.

Or the beginning.

Mud shoved aside the random thought. The second the pastor announced the end of the service he grabbed Amelia's hand. "Ready to go?"

"Sure." She looked at him, her head tilted a little to one side. "Are you okay?"

"Fine." He pressed his lips together. He just wanted to get out of there. "Can we go back to your place for lunch?" As much as he loved hanging out with Nick and Vi, he wasn't in the mood for a crowd.

Back at Amelia's place she set about making salad sandwiches. They were delicious. "You've done something special," he drawled. It was a hint from an Aussie movie, but it would probably go over her head.

She rolled her eyes heavenward. "It's only a sandwich."

"Still ..." he decided against explaining. He would show her the movie instead.

"Any plans for this afternoon?"

He shrugged. "Not really. We can hang out and watch a movie if you like."

Her lips curved upward. "One of my favorite pastimes."

Once they'd cleaned up from lunch, he found a streamed version of *The Castle,* the movie he'd thought about. "This is a classic Aussie film. You might not get the humor, but then again you might surprise me. I hope you enjoy it."

Amelia snuggled up next to him, her head resting on his shoulder and his arm slung around her, breathing her in. This ... this felt like home.

CHAPTER FIFTEEN

Amelia rested against Mud, trying to make sense of the movie. Mud laughed now and then, leaving her wondering what was so funny. Until a scene came with a family dinner and a bowl of ice cream, which the lead character thought was amazing. She sat up straight and looked at him. "Oh. I see. The sandwich."

"You got it." Mud looked like a cat who'd found a bathtub full of cream. He brushed a few strands of hair back from her face. "You're so beautiful."

Amelia's heart skittered at those words. He pulled her back toward him and tilted her face up, his thumb caressing her cheek. Amelia shifted, turned more fully toward him as he pressed his lips to hers. The fire and intensity in his kisses were unmistakable as he tightened his embrace and she responded in kind. He began nuzzling her neck, sending shivers of delight through her.

"Hold me, Meels," he whispered between kisses. "I need you so much."

Suddenly, everything within Amelia went cold. Shut

down. Full stop like a car skidding on the freeway to avoid an accident. Gasping, she pulled away from him and stood up, straightening her clothes as if she were trying to straighten her jack-knifed emotions. "I think you should go."

Mud wore a look of deep shock then confusion. "What's wrong?"

But those words echoed around and around her brain. *I need you. I need you. I need you.* Dread curled her stomach. "Just go."

He reached out a hand to her. "We don't have to—"

"Please. Go." She picked up a cushion and hugged it to her stomach, her eyes burning with tears that would no doubt flow within minutes. Why did he have to say that?

Mud's brow furrowed. "Fine. Whatever." He grabbed his keys and wallet with agitated movements and headed for the door. But he paused with his hand on the doorknob. "Aren't you even going to tell me what this is about?"

Amelia sank onto the sofa, covering her face, but she shook her head. She couldn't. He would probably never understand it anyway. Seconds later the door slammed and she was alone with her tormented thoughts.

How could she ever explain how those three words triggered a thousand flashbacks. Recalling every request Pa had ever made—demands made with no consideration of her feelings or capacity? And more memories of Cody and all his "needs" flooded her. She simply did not want to be needed. Ever. Again.

If only Mud had stopped at "you're so beautiful." She wanted to be loved and desired, not clung to out of desperation. And that was the truth. Mud sounded desperate. If she gave in to his needs even once, he would undoubtedly ask for more and more, expecting her to sacrifice until she had nothing left of herself.

More memories surfaced. Of a time when she'd been sick with a fever and chest infection, but for whatever reason, Pa never saw it. He continued to demand his dinner, glasses of water, to fetch whatever he needed, leaving her to wonder who would ever take care of her. She'd dragged herself around, pushing herself to do chores when all she wanted was to curl up in bed. And all she earned was the title of being independent and a trooper. But she never wanted those labels. Instead, she wanted to be heard, seen, valued. She never wanted to feel that way again.

Amelia threw herself back against the armrest of the sofa where minutes ago she'd snuggled with Mud. Why, oh why, had she allowed herself to become attached? To Mud, of all people. Because he was the last person she thought would be needy. Hadn't he always been the carefree one?

Oh, she'd been blind for sure. His brother had died and he was grieving. Of course he wasn't going to be the same old devil-may-care guy from last year. Amelia groaned and hugged the cushion tighter. He'd even told her he would change. But to become needy and clingy? No, she couldn't stomach it.

She threw the cushion across the room, got up and stormed to her room, wishing she'd never met Mud Murchison.

———

MUD STOOD under the shower at the gym, still wondering what had gone wrong. He pumped up the cold-water pressure hoping it would cool him down. Overheated from the extreme workout, yes, but also from the words burning in his head. *Just go.*

No explanation. No apology. Just an order to leave.

Which sent him straight to the gym and a high-intensity training session, followed by a long run on the treadmill. Even all that exercise hadn't taken the edge off. The one person who'd brought a level of solace to his world had cut him off. Shut him down. Kicked him out.

A vice squeezed his heart making it hard to breathe. He shut off the shower faucet and toweled off. Mud considered sending a message to Amelia but had no idea of what to say. It would either be a string of angry words or something akin to begging. And he wasn't that desperate. It was humiliating enough to have her reject him so suddenly. He didn't need to add to his chagrin by playing the fool.

Had he been wrong about her the whole time? As he traced back through their times together, he realized she had never overtly told him how she felt about him. Her words were more repeats of what he'd said, or simple "me toos." Perhaps she wasn't as sure about him as he was about her.

Mud grabbed his gym bag and stalked out to his car. How was he ever going to sleep tonight? He drove around town for a while looking for anything that might pique his interest. Nothing. He drove to Andy O'Dell's house to see if he might learn anything new. Nothing. He drove to the bridge and stood on the concrete balustrade again to relive that sense of adrenaline pumping. Nothing.

Disgusted with himself, he finally headed home. Nick took one look at him and said, "What's up, bro? You okay?"

"I don't wanna talk about it." Mud dropped his gym bag near the washing machine so he wouldn't forget to take care of it.

Nick followed him, staring. "Did something happen with Amelia?"

How insightful of him. "I said I don't wanna talk about it." Mud headed to the kitchen to find a drink. Cola, water, coffee? Something stronger would be preferable, but there wasn't any beer in the fridge. He picked up a cola then thought better. He already knew he wouldn't sleep. Why make it worse? Instead, he fetched a glass and filled it with water.

He turned to see Nick leaning against the counter behind him, eyes narrowed, ready to pounce. Better switch topics now before his friend started poking and prodding.

"Hey, you wanna go rock climbing tomorrow?"

Nick watched him intently for a moment then moved to grab his own glass of water. "Tomorrow's Monday."

"And?" Mud shrugged. He cared nothing for real life demands at this moment.

"Some of us have to work."

"Whatever." Mud pushed away from the bench and headed to his room. "I'll go on my own."

Nick's sigh was audible behind him. "Alright. I'll see what I can do."

———

Before Amelia knew it, Thursday afternoon rolled around and it was time to take Violet and their other close friends to Soap Lake. Between avoiding Mud and avoiding Violet's probing questions, it was a wonder she managed to get ready for the weekend away at all.

It wasn't like she could deny anything was wrong. Nick and Vi seemed to talk about everything and therefore, within twenty-four hours, Violet learned Mud had become sullen. And since Amelia probably displayed signs of moodiness, despite trying not to, and neither Nick nor Vi lacked intelligence, they correctly deduced something had happened between her and Mud.

Of course that meant that Vi brought Mud up in conversation repeatedly.

"Did you hear Nick and Mud went rock climbing yesterday?" was one attempt.

"Sounds like fun." Amelia kept her eyes on her computer screen.

"You weren't invited?"

Amelia had lifted her left shoulder. "Why would I be?"

Thankfully, most of her curt responses ended the conversations quickly. Or else Amelia changed the subject to some detail about the wedding, which was always a sure way to distract Violet.

But now? Now they were sitting in the car together for two and a half hours on their way to Soap Lake. The other girls had taken their own cars because of different work shifts and planned to meet them at the resort. Now there was no escaping Violet's interrogation.

"Alright girl. Spill," Vi said as soon as they were out of town.

Amelia rolled her eyes. She should have taken Tony up on the offer to drive them. But no, she'd insisted on driving her best friend to her bachelorette weekend. Besides, it saved him from making two trips.

"Spill what?" Amelia feigned ignorance.

"What's going on with you and Mud?"

As if pretending to be innocent would work. "Nothing." Denial was the next best thing. Amelia kept her eyes on the road, dead ahead.

"Come on." Vi slapped her knees, clearly losing patience. "You've been tense all week, and from what I hear, so has Mud. So give over and tell me."

Amelia shrugged. "Seriously. It's nothing." Well, Vi would likely consider it a tidal wave in a teacup.

Vi pressed her lips together and let out a brief huff. "Don't you want to get it out of your system now so we can enjoy the weekend?"

When she put it like that ...

Amelia chewed on her bottom lip. She didn't want to ruin Vi's bachelorette party with her sour grapes, lemon juice, vinegar inspired disposition.

"Did you two break up or something?" Vi pressed.

"No." The denial came out quickly. But then, "maybe." She hadn't actually thought of it in those terms, and considering she still squirmed at the thought of that moment ...

"What did he do?" Vi frowned.

"Nothing." Amelia mumbled. She would wear that word out in a minute if Violet kept up with the questions.

"Did he cheat?"

"No." Amelia answered firmly, her heart still finding defense for him despite her sentiments. "And it's not like we were that serious anyway."

"Did he ..." Vi hesitated. "Did he forc—?"

"No. Vi." Amelia cut her off, shocked at her friend's line of thought. "No. Nothing like that."

"Well, what then?" Vi lifted her hands, nonplussed. "Is it something you can work out? Because the wedding is a week away and you two are our key people."

Tears pricked at Amelia's eyes. She didn't want to be a Debbie-Downer for Violet or for Nick, or for their wedding. She swallowed hard. "It's just..." She shook her head. "I can't." Amelia shifted her blurry gaze to Violet and back to the road as she swiped at her eyes. "I thought I could do this relation-ship thing but I can't." Not while she was in danger of losing herself again.

"Are you saying you're the problem, not Mud?"

Amelia bit down on her lip and nodded. That was the

truth. Because apart from that clingy side he'd shown, he was near perfect.

———

MUD SAT in church with his arms folded across his chest. Why had he even agreed to come with Nick? Wasn't he unworthy enough already? Every time he went he ended up feeling worse than before. And yet, something kept bringing him back. Perhaps it was the sense of hope in the air. Hope and life. Two things sadly lacking in his world.

At the end of the service Nick turned to him. "What's going on, bro? You've been shutting me out all week."

And just like that, something snapped within. "Nothing's working." His shoulders slumped forward and his throat strangled. Mud balled his hand into a fist and pounded it into his thigh. He was so sick of these emotions.

"What do you mean?" Nick placed a hand on his shoulder, concern and friendship in his eyes.

"Things need to change. I can't keep going like this. But everything I do, everything I try, either doesn't work or falls to pieces."

Nick squeezed his shoulder. "I can see how hard you've been trying and that's awesome. But you don't have to do it all on your own."

"What do you mean?" Mud wiped at his moist cheeks.

"I think you know what I mean." Nick's eyes crinkled at the corners. "You've been reading the Bible, and you've listened to me, the pastor, Brandon—all of us—saying Jesus is the one who can help you. And I suspect you've heard Him calling you, too."

Mud swallowed, the truth winging through his soul.

"All you have to do is stop fighting Him and let Him in.

The Bible says, 'Come to me, all you who are weary and burdened, and I will give you rest. Take my yoke upon you and learn from me, for I am gentle and humble in heart, and you will find rest for your souls. For my yoke is easy and my burden is light.'"

Rest for your soul.

Oh, how Mud needed that. Something within him gave in. Like walls crashing down in a demolition. "What do I need to do?"

Such a simple statement. But Nick threw his arms around him in a bear hug. "Mate." His voice cracked. "You have just made my day."

Nick led him to the pastor and together they talked and prayed. And oh what a profound prayer. Mud acknowledged all of his selfish, sinful life and handed it over to the Lord for forgiveness. He was ready to live however Jesus said he should. Crazy. It was like a weight lifted off him. He hadn't been this light since … since he couldn't remember. He even laughed.

He and Nick headed home after that and talked for hours about this new life he'd chosen. Eventually Mud raised the topic that still stung. "What do I do about Amelia?"

Nick put down the pen he'd been fiddling with and looked at him. "What happened with her?"

"I really don't know, man." No matter how many times Mud replayed that moment, he couldn't figure out what went wrong.

"Well, tell me about it. Sometimes talking it out brings things to light."

"Okay." Mud sighed. "We were watching a movie on the sofa, and then we were making out, and she suddenly stood up and told me to get out." Mud shrugged. "I mean, that's literally what happened. No explanation or anything."

"Hmm." Nick frowned, then cleared his throat. "You weren't pressuring her to … you know … were you?"

"Nah man." If he didn't know Nick so well, he would take offence at the suggestion. "I would never. I mean, it was getting heavy, but she was into it, too. At least I thought she was." Mud's voice trailed off as he tried to remember again. No. Until that moment, she'd been kissing him with the same level of passion.

"Did you say something that might have offended her?" Nick seemed almost as confused as him.

Mud wracked his brain again and shrugged. "I was looking for some comfort. I was miserable after talking to Mum and thinking about Griff again."

Nick picked up the pen again and spun it around his fingers, but then gave him a direct look. "I'm gonna give you some advice. You mightn't like it but it's important."

Mud looked at him warily. "Here it comes. Okay, shoot."

"Try not to use Amelia to meet your needs. Or anything else, for that matter." He glanced at an empty beer bottle. "Start going to the Lord when you need comfort or peace."

Mud narrowed his eyes. "Right. How do I do that?"

"Pray. Read the Bible. Listen to worship music. All those things work for me." Nick tapped his Bible. "And as for Amelia, try showing her you value her, treat her as a precious gift. Assuming you do still want to continue the relationship, that is."

Mud studied his friend. Why had he never listened to Nick's wisdom over the years? Probably would have saved himself a lot of hot water if he had. "Yeah, I do. And treating her like a treasure will be easy—if I can even get her to talk to me."

CHAPTER SIXTEEN

The weekend in Soap Lake was relaxing on the whole, with fireworks over the lake, pampering by massage, sauna and spa. Violet thanked Amelia effusively when they drove back to Trinity Lakes. Bree had been frosty towards Amelia at first but mellowed when she learned there was trouble between her and Mud. After that she was all sympathy. Not that Amelia told her any details. Bree simply made assumptions which Amelia didn't bother to correct.

Bree probably thought Mud had heartlessly dumped her. The truth was more the opposite, but since he hadn't even reached out to Amelia in the last week, she didn't think it necessary to set Bree straight. Besides, divulging that it was she who called things off would mean trying to explain her dread of being swallowed up by need. The fear she still couldn't get past. The fear that niggled at her every waking thought. Every time Mud's gorgeous face popped into her mind, so did the panic.

Especially now that he'd suddenly started texting her again.

Hey, can we talk?

Amelia groaned internally. This week already promised to be a doozy with final wedding plans in full swing. She darted from place to place, sorting all the finer details from her five-mile-long list of errands.

Her phone chimed again as she left the printers with an armload of wedding programs and place cards. Amelia fumbled with the parcels and her keys, trying to check the message. Her eyebrows lifted in surprise. This one was from Nick.

Hi Amelia. I need a favor from you.

She unlocked her car, put the packages in and typed a reply.

What's up?

Could you help me get a surprise ready for Violet?

Of course.

Happy to help.

Another ping sounded on her phone as she sat in her car.

Please.

Mud. She tossed the phone onto the passenger seat and drove to the nearest gift store to pick up an order. Violet had organized small thankyou presents for everyone in her bridal party, which was a lovely gesture.

As she stood at the counter waiting for the order, her phone pinged once more. And again, it was Mud.

I need to see you. We need to talk.

Amelia sighed as she shoved her phone into her purse, collected the bags, and returned to her car. Maybe he was right. She shook her head. She didn't have time right now. Time to go back to the office and make a load of confirmation phone calls. This time her phone rang. Violet.

"Hi."

"Hey, where are you at?"

"About to finish up here. On my way back to you now."

"Great. Can you stop by Becky's coffee cart? I need a coffee."

In that moment something snapped. This was all too much. "What about what *I* need?" The words fairly exploded from her. "You need me. Mud needs me. Even Nick needs me. It's exhausting."

Stunned silence for a few heartbeats and Amelia put her head in her hands, cringing internally.

"Hey, I didn't mean to overload you." Vi's voice was quiet, hesitant. "Don't worry about coffee. Come back here and we can talk about it. We can offload some of your tasks."

Amelia tipped her eyes to the roof of her car. The last thing she wanted to do was talk, but she'd done it now. Blown her top. "It's fine. I'm sorry. I'll get the coffee." And she hung up.

Her spirits were heavy as she waited for Becky to make the coffee, even though the barista chatted excitedly about the big wedding in a few days. Amelia merely nodded and forced a smile.

Back at the office, Violet immediately sat her down on the lounge and gazed at her with concern. "What's going on? Am I working you too hard?"

Amelia shook her head. "Not really. It's not about you. I'm happy to do all this for you, you know that, right?"

"You said Nick needed you too?" Vi's brows furrowed.

Amelia chewed her lip. "That was a secret. It's nothing worth me biting your head off for, or his."

Violet's head tilted to one side. "Is this about Mud?"

"I guess." Amelia shrugged. She might as well spit it out. "It's just … lately … I keep hearing my dad's voice in my head."

Violet's brows creased again. "Your dad?"

"When he was sick," Amelia explained. "It was 'Amelia, get this', or 'Amelia, do that'." Her voice broke and tears formed on her lashes. "I had to do *everything* for him. And there was no one to look after me."

"Oh, hon." Violet scooted over and wrapped her up in a tender hug. "I'm so sorry. I haven't taken the time to check in on you. You always seem so independent and strong."

"I never wanted to be so independent," Amelia whispered. "But I had no choice."

Vi looked directly into her eyes. "What happened with your dad is not normal. You understand that, don't you? I would class it as neglect to be honest."

The truth of those words hit home and Amelia sobbed. It was as though in that moment all her pain was validated— seen and understood.

"No one should have to be left without being cared for. That was a complete imbalance and damaging to your self-worth."

Amelia only nodded. How long had she believed she was unimportant? Mom didn't care enough to stay and Pa was only interested in his own needs. Violet's words hit on every open wound and though Amelia cried uncontrollably, there was a sense of relief in having it out in the open.

When the sobs finally subsided and Amelia wiped her face and blew her nose, Violet smiled at her. "You know it's actually okay to lean on others sometimes. The Lord made us in community so we can support one another. But it is a two-way street. And when us faulty humans can't suffice, Jesus can. He loves you, Amelia." A tear slipped down Violet's face. "Loves you like you can't even begin to comprehend."

Amelia nodded, still blinking back tears. Without even asking, Violet had answered the questions which had plagued her since first going back to church. Her parents did *not* show love as per the Bible's definition, but there was a dependable, fulfilling kind of love available. Question was, could she let go of her fears and accept it, or learn to trust it? She let out a wobbly breath. Perhaps it was time to start.

"Is that what happened with Mud?" Violet straightened on the sofa. "Did his needs become too much for you?"

"Yeah." Amelia swallowed. "I freaked out. I couldn't … can't go there again."

Vi reached over and squeezed her hand. "This is probably a season for him. He's grieving. Like I said before, it's okay to lean on each other. And there will be times you need to lean on someone else, like you did after the accident. Yes?"

When she put it like that, how could Amelia argue? It seemed completely fair. Wholesome even. She had to admit it would be wonderful to be in a partnership with the equal give and take of meeting and fulfilling needs. Was it possible to have that with Mud? Had all of this been an over-the-top reaction because of her past experiences? If so, she owed Mud a conversation at the very least. She picked up her phone and waved it before Violet. "You're right. And I probably should reply to Mud." Before she got up, though, she threw her arms around Violet as gratitude flooded her. "Thank you for being the best friend ever."

———

FINALLY, a notification from Amelia popped up on Mud's screen. He breathed out audibly with relief, and just as quickly his shoulders sagged with disappointment.

Can we talk after the wedding? Swamped with prep. Sorry.

Mud gritted his teeth. That was two days away. But at least she sounded amenable and there was the hint of apology there … he supposed. He really didn't want there to be awkwardness between them on Nick's big day. He typed an argument then remembered his conversations with Nick and backspaced.

Anything I can do to help?

He waited a few minutes until an answer popped up.

Thanks for the offer. I think I'm OK. Unless you want to stand in for me at the hairdresser and get a stunning updo while I sleep in?

Mud snickered. That sounded more like the Amelia he'd grown to care about. Though he hoped she wasn't sweeping everything under the rug.

I'd hate to upstage you. As if that were even possible. He added a laughing emoji as his grin spread. *But if that's what it takes …* He wanted her to know he was serious, that he would do anything for her, even if this was in joke form.

When no reply came, he worried he'd overstepped. He speed typed another message.

Can I ask one thing? Is it over between us?

This time it was half an hour or more before her answer pinged on his phone. Heart hammering, he opened the text.

I thought you'd want nothing to do with me after I cut you off and ghosted you like that. Maybe you still won't after I tell you everything.

That wasn't a no. But it wasn't a yes either. And her actions had badly hurt and confused him, and still no clarity on what he'd done wrong. Nothing would move until they'd had that talk. Time to call a truce.

OK. No pressure. For the sake of the wedding, though, can we be friends?

Her reply came swiftly. *Of course. Definitely.*

That brought a level of relief, although saying no pressure was easier said than done. Mud craved seeing her, interacting with her. Thankfully, he had plenty to focus on with

Nick's preparations. That evening would be the buck's night concert to attend along with a few of Nick's new American friends.

Mud had never been to a Christian concert before, but with his new decision in hand, he found himself caught up in the worshipful atmosphere. His throat constricted once again, and he whispered thanks to God who had so graciously taken his burdens.

After the concert the group found a late-night bowling alley and played a few games, fed themselves with burgers and headed back to Trinity Lakes in the early hours. Nick seemed to enjoy himself, and slapped Mud on the back with a "thanks bro," several times.

But Mud struggled to focus on anything, his thoughts drifting to Amelia time after time. These last few days had finally given him some clarity on moving forward, but more than ever he needed to share those thoughts with her. It was hard to wait so long before he could get it off his chest. And he didn't know what she would think of his new ideas. But he would see her at the rehearsal dinner and wondered what to do to show her he treasured her, without coming on too strong.

The next afternoon, on the way to the gardens by Lake Wainscott, Mud pulled over in front of the shops in main street. "Do you mind if we stop?" he asked Nick. "I'd like to get some flowers for Amelia."

The corner of Nick's mouth curved up. "Great idea. I'll get some for Vi, too."

They entered the florist's and Nick immediately aimed for the red roses. Mud hesitated and the lady at the counter offered to help.

"I'm looking for something that says 'you're special.'" He winced, unsure if she would catch his meaning.

The lady nodded. "If you have a few minutes, I can make something up for you."

"Awesome." Mud shoved his hands in his pockets, then stood by to watch as she worked. The florist deftly pulled together different blooms in purple and yellow with green foliage and delicate white flowers filling the gaps. Mud had no idea what they were but they looked good.

She glanced up at him and smiled. "Yellow is often used for friendship, and purple can be admiration and also royalty." She winked at him. "That's pretty special, don't you agree?"

"Perfect." Mud returned her grin. Who knew if Amelia was aware of the secret code to flower colors? Hopefully she would get the gist. He looked over his shoulder at Nick, who had completed his purchase and waited patiently by the door.

A few minutes later he'd paid for the bouquet and headed back to the car.

"So, have you two made up?" Nick asked as they drove the short distance to the parking lot by the lake.

"Well, let's just say the lines of communication are open." Mud jerked his thumb toward the floral arrangement on the back seat. "Trying to follow your advice, bro."

Nick gave him a friendly punch on the arm. "Good for you. I'm sure she'll appreciate the gesture."

Before they got out of the car, Nick put a staying hand on his shoulder. "Are you all good? I mean, how are you going with the Griff stuff and everything? Will you be okay after I leave for my honeymoon tomorrow?"

Mud drew in a deep breath and thought about it for a moment. "You know, I'm more settled than I've been in a long time. I think I'll be fine." It was true. Ever since deciding to give it all to Jesus, peace had rested on him. "And if I go downhill, I can always talk to Brandon."

Nick nodded, patting his shoulder. "And the Lord. Don't forget to talk to Him."

"Of course."

"Okay. Let's do this." Nick put his arm up for a fist bump and Mud responded.

Mud noticed Nick's bouquet still on the back seat as he locked the car. "Aren't you bringing your flowers?"

"I'll give Vi hers later." He shoved Mud. "You can be the hero for now."

Suddenly, Mud's mouth went dry. Nerves had never been a thing for him, especially with girls, but now his hand trembled around the rather public expression in his hands. No, it wasn't roses declaring undying love or anything, but still…

He approached Amelia hesitantly, ignoring the others milling around, and tried to form his mouth into a smile, which probably looked more like a grimace the way his lips quivered. And it didn't help that her eyes were on him, an uncertain expression on her face.

"Hey Meels. These are for you," was all he managed in a whisper, then swallowed the thick ball in his throat.

Their fingers brushed as she took the bouquet, sending shivers up his arm, and he shoved his hands in his pockets.

"Thank you." A simple response with a shy smile and a gaze which dropped to the grass. "They're beautiful."

Just like you. The words were on the tip of his tongue, but he held them back.

"Now you're all here, let's get started." The pastor clapped and motioned the bridal party closer.

Mud breathed out, the awkward moment passing. The busyness of rehearsing a wedding kept them mostly separated until they practiced the recessional. Arm in arm, he walked Amelia down the aisle between chairs that awaited some bridal decorations. "You're going to be amazing tomorrow," he murmured as they followed Nick and Vi.

"Do you mean to say I'm not amazing now?"

Although she fixed her eyes on the couple ahead of them, Mud recognized the amusement in her voice. What to say? He was in danger of saying something too intense, so he laughed softly instead. Truly, he thought her stunning now. How would he survive her in full bridesmaid array?

Before he knew it, they were all headed to the old boathouse for the rehearsal dinner. The bridal party plus close family members all mingled, ate and laughed together from a casual buffet. It was great to see Nick's family had arrived and Mud enjoyed catching up with them. Of course they all gave him condolences about Griff, but thankfully no one focused on that tragedy. Mud didn't want to dwell on his grief during his best friend's wedding.

Mostly, he kept his distance from Amelia during the evening, even though he itched to be near her. He knew he wouldn't be able to maintain trivial conversation for long. He caught her gaze on him several times and this delightful exchange would have to suffice. It wasn't a late night as the bride and bridesmaids had an early start ahead of them.

When they'd said their goodbyes, Nick walked with Violet, and Mud joined them, walking with Amelia to the car.

"You all set?" They approached the limo that waited for them.

"I think so," Amelia replied.

"She'd better be," Violet laughed. "I'm relying on her tomorrow." Nick tugged her hand and led her around to the other side of the stretch limo, where they were soon locked in an embrace.

"Not too nervous?" Mud continued his check in with Amelia.

"Not too nervous." Amelia placed her purse and bouquet on the seat and straightened again. "Thanks again for the flowers. It was very thoughtful."

"Well, you're worth it." Mud squeezed one of her hands gently and let it go again as she sat in the car. "See you tomorrow." He gently closed the door and watched as the car drove away, Nick coming to stand with him.

"All good?" Nick asked.

"All good." Mud slapped him on the back. "Let's see if we can disperse this mob so we can get some rest, too."

CHAPTER SEVENTEEN

Amelia stood with all the guests and waved as the newlyweds drove away in Nick's flash pickup truck, off to their honeymoon in the wilds of Canada. And with them drove most of Amelia's busyness and obligations. Violet had told her to have a week off.

She watched the empty road, reflecting on the beautiful ceremony and the joyful reception. Everything had gone off without a hitch. Tears flowed, both as they exchanged vows, and when Nick sang to Violet at the wedding feast. Amelia sighed. It couldn't have gone any better. Except perhaps if she were on more than simple speaking terms with Mud.

In a midnight blue tux, he was more gorgeous than ever. And the way he'd looked at her when she preceded Violet down the aisle, well, anyone would have thought Amelia was the bride. His mouth dropped open and unbridled admiration shone from his eyes. Amelia had chewed the inside of her lip trying not to smile.

In traditional wedding form, they sat together at the dinner, but any conversations they shared were stilted or interrupted prematurely. Of course, as soon as Nick and Vi had completed their bridal waltz, the happy couple waved Mud and Amelia to join them on the dance floor. The fact it was a slow, romantic dance made her both uneasy and thrilled at the same time.

Being in Mud's arms, swaying to music, seemed like the most natural place to be. His arms snug around her waist, his eyes like firebrands burning into hers as he softly sung along to the old Bryan Adams song, *Everything I Do*. Way to make her insides flop over in a three-sixty somersault. Was he trying to tell her that's how he felt?

"So, when are we gonna have this talk, Meels?" he asked as the song died down.

"Tonight," she whispered as she withdrew her hands from behind his neck. "As soon as this is all over, I promise."

"That might be very late." He grasped her hand.

"It doesn't matter." She shook her head. There was too much tension, too much uncertainty between them. "Even if it's three A.M."

The celebrations separated them again as they mingled with guests. She was surprised when Bree flopped down beside her at one point.

"You know, I wanted to be angry with you and Mud." Straight to the heart of it. No beating around the bush.

Amelia turned to her with eyebrows raised. "But?"

"Watching you two together … I …" Bree shrugged. "You've got something I never had with him."

"What do you mean?"

"The way he's been looking at you all day. I'm pretty sure he never looked at me that way." Bree released a little sigh. Was that jealousy? Disappointment? Something else? Amelia had never analyzed how Mud looked at her, except that it made her feel like the only person in existence on the planet.

She would be stupid to throw that away because of fear, wouldn't she?

Bree took Amelia's hands in hers and looked earnestly at her. "Anyway, I wanted to tell you I'm not holding any grudges. I hope it really works out for you both."

"Thanks Bree." Amelia pulled her friend in for a hug. "And I hope for the best for you and your new boyfriend too."

"Yeah, thanks." Bree smiled again and moved off to talk to someone else.

So, now with the newlyweds gone, and most of the guests dispersing, it was time to seek Mud. Amelia entered the massive marquee Morgan Reynolds had set up at a local vineyard, with views over grape vines, a river snaking through a valley, and the mountains in the distance. He'd paid an exorbitant amount to the winery owners to take over their property for the day. Then brought in a selected chef to cater and set up an amazing venue for his daughter. She checked her phone. Not three A.M., only twenty minutes past eleven.

She glanced around to see Mud saying his farewells to Nick's family, embracing each one. He saw her standing there and nodded slightly. As soon as he finished he headed to her. "You're a bit early." He looked at his watch. "It's nowhere near three."

"I can go—" Amelia turned away, but he grabbed her arm.

"Not on your life."

She giggled. "Shall we go outside? The stars are beautiful tonight."

"Sounds perfect."

Mud entwined his fingers through hers as he led her out into the coolness of the summer evening, and she had no inclination to pull away from him. She tugged him towards a romantic swing for two which stood in the garden.

"It was a lovely wedding, wasn't it?" she asked as they sat on the swaying bench together.

"The best."

They sat in silence for a few minutes, listening to night birds and the creaking of the ropes as the swing gently rocked. Amelia needed to work up the courage to say what she needed to say. She kicked off her heels and tucked her aching feet onto the cushioned seat beneath her, turning slightly toward him.

"Did I do something wrong?" Mud's eyes were wide as their gaze locked.

"No." She glanced down at their hands clasped together. "I owe you an apology. You've shared so much of your history with me, but I've held most of mine back. You deserve to hear my story." With a deep breath she told of her ordeal with her mother and father, and how it had affected her response to his grief and need for support. "I was scared and overwhelmed. I just … I shut down. I'm so sorry, Mud. I never meant to hurt you." Tears beaded on her lashes and she blinked them back.

"Hey, hey, it's okay." Mud's voice was like a caress, as gentle as his hands that now cupped her face. "I also need to apologize. I never wanted you to feel like I was taking advantage of you or using you to make myself feel better." His thumbs wiped at her tears. "I'm learning to lean on something greater, on a powerful and loving God, in fact."

Amelia blinked again. "Really?"

"Yeah." Mud chuckled softly. "I've finally seen the light. It's taken me far too many years and I've made far too many mistakes."

Amelia shifted to put her head on his shoulder, and his

arm immediately tucked around hers. "I'm learning that it's okay for people to lean on each other from time to time." She shuddered. It was still a huge thing to say. They rocked the swing in silence again for a moment.

"I've been thinking about the future a lot in the past two weeks." Mud eventually broke the silence.

"Yeah?"

"I've figured out what I want to do now." His voice was barely above a whisper, and she could feel his heart pounding beneath her cheek. "For almost a decade I've been jumping from one job, one occupation, to another, always trying to find meaning but never finding it. I want to make a difference in people's lives, help people. But I can't go back to firefighting. I'm considering going home to Australia and studying to be a nurse."

Amelia sat bolt upright and stared at him, one word branding itself in her mind like a hot iron. "Australia? You're leaving?" A ball swelled in her throat and her lips quivered.

Mud's eyes were wide, wide and sad, and his voice cracked. "My family needs me, Meels."

Amelia scrambled for any sensible thought, but only one surfaced. "But what about us?"

He grabbed her hands and offered a wobbly smile. "You could come with me."

Amelia yanked her hands free and stood up from the swing, anger and hurt rising. "My whole life is here."

Mud hung his head, his shoulders slumped. "I don't know what else to say. I just know what I have to do."

Amelia grabbed her discarded shoes and swung away from him. "I knew this would happen. Thanks for nothing." She stormed away. How did he expect her to drop everything and run after him? And not even a word from him about love or commitment. No promises for the future. There was nothing to hang her hopes on. She found Tony and managed to get into his car before the tears flowed freely.

———

MUD STAYED on the swing for a long time, his mood sinking like lead weights in the ocean. Once again he'd messed up. Especially after Amelia told him how her father had drained everything she had. Now he'd made it sound like she should give up everything for him. He hadn't thought before he'd spoken, compelled to lay the truth out there.

It was the right thing for him to go back to Australia and support Mum. And the inspiration to study nursing came from the experience of caring for Amelia right after the hit-and-run. Compassion came to him easily. After some more therapy for himself, he could specialize in mental health, help others through similar trauma to what he'd been through.

These new ideas excited him and he wanted to share them with Amelia. Wanted her to be a part of it all. Mud punched his fist into his thigh and groaned. Now she saw him as another selfish guy who only cared about his own needs. But that wasn't who he was. Well, not any more. Somehow he had to show her he wanted her best as well.

One of the pack-up crew found him some time later and approached hesitantly. "Sorry, sir, um, we really need to dismantle this swing."

Mud checked his watch and humphed. It was nearly three now. Had he been mulling that long? He got up from the swing and gave the worker a thumbs up. "No probs, man. I should've gone home a long time ago."

He trudged to his car and drove the half hour back to Trinity Lakes and a quiet flat with no Nick to talk to, and

Manny was long asleep. Mud considered the gaming console, but for the first time in a long time, decided against it. Even if sleep made itself elusive, he was determined to try.

In the end he slept past his alarm and missed church, but an idea had formed in his head during the night. If he exposed the hit-and-run driver so Amelia saw justice done, wouldn't that take a weight off her mind? Show her he cared about her wellbeing? And with the wedding behind them, he could put one hundred percent effort into the search.

Mud sent a message to Brandon to see if he'd learned the name of O'Dell's girlfriend from his friends in the education field, and before long he sat down with his laptop to search Kathleen Jackson's social media accounts. Within half an hour, he'd jotted down several details about her and saved a photo of her to his phone. But the details raised more questions.

Kathleen was a student from a college in Walla Walla. Had she been in Trinity Lakes recently? If they were a couple, it was more than possible. Had they met on campus? A check on O'Dell's socials revealed that he, too, had studied in Walla Walla in the past year or so.

Strangely, though, Kathleen had posted to her social account frequently until about three months ago, then nothing. What did that mean? Had something happened? Perhaps the hit-and-run. He rechecked the dates. No, she stopped posting well before the accident.

Mud still pondered over these things as he arrived at the garage. This would be his last week helping at the auto shop. With the wedding over, there was nothing keeping him in Trinity Lakes. Nothing except Amelia, and other than finding this hit-and-run driver, he had no idea of how to move forward with her. It was unfair to expect her to give up her whole life to move to Australia, but he knew he must go home. It seemed they were at a stale-mate, and although he'd sent her a message of apology, he was lost for what else to say. Her responses were stilted.

Problem was, he hadn't booked a ticket home either. Every time he got to the confirmation page, he couldn't go through with it. Mud rubbed his face as he searched for a multi-meter to test the car's battery. Great. He'd probably smeared grease all over his cheek.

"What's eating you today?" Brandon must have noticed his furrowed brow.

Mud grabbed a rag and wiped his face. Where to start? Something less serious, perhaps. "I might miss working with you, Mac."

"Are you going home? When?" Brandon sounded disappointed.

"I told Bruce this morning. Next week." Even though he had no ticket yet.

"You don't seem too excited about it."

Insightful as ever. Mud pressed his lips together and fiddled with the leads of the multi-meter. Brandon's eyebrows raised.

"Oh. Your girl. You don't want to leave her."

"Got it in one." Mud blew the top of his index finger like a smoking gun. Huh. It dawned on him he'd never had trouble leaving a woman before. "I'm not ready for this to be over."

"Why does it have to be over? Do you love her?" Brandon's keen eyes watched him intently.

"More than anything." Oh, man. That was the first time he'd admitted that out loud. "But she doesn't want to come with me, and I need to go home."

Brandon put down his tools and came to stand next to Mud, who leaned against a workbench. "Does she know you love her?"

"Well, yeah. I think so." Mud rubbed his brow, suddenly unsure. "I mean, the chemistry is off the charts. You'd have to be blind to say there's nothing there."

Brandon folded his arms across his chest. "Let me get this straight. You're letting the 'chemistry' do all the talking. I assume that means making out, right? But you haven't actually told her you love her."

"I ... I didn't want her to get her hopes up when I couldn't even see my own future." Mud shrugged.

"And you think dating her, kissing her, spending all your spare time with her, wouldn't get her hopes up?" Brandon's face looked grim.

Mud winced. He'd done it again. Taken advantage of their mutual attraction, making no commitment first. He put his hands over his face. "You're right. I'm such a loser."

Brandon squeezed his shoulder. "Hey, it's not the end of the world, Mud. I'm sure you can make this right."

"How? She hates me for sure now."

"Two things." Brandon held up two fingers. "Tell her how you feel and what you want your future with her to look like. And pray. God has a way of changing people's hearts." He chuckled. "But do the praying first."

"Thanks Mac," Mud said with dry sarcasm. "It's *my* heart that needs changing. Is that what you reckon?"

Brandon pushed away from the bench to continue his work. "No. I reckon the Lord needs to be our first go-to in every situation."

"Fair enough." Mud nodded, although his first thought was probably true. He needed God to change his heart and give him the right motives before approaching Amelia again.

"Hey, did you ever find out any more about that hit-and-run?" Brandon asked as he used a wrench to unfasten a nut.

Mud rubbed the back of his neck. "We really only have

guesses at this point. We suspect Andy O'Dell's girlfriend was driving, but we have no proof. Short of confronting them, I'm out of ideas."

Brandon paused and looked up at him. "You're not actually going to do that though, are you?"

Mud shrugged. He neither wanted to confirm nor deny.

"I mean, let's say you're right. For whatever reason they've covered this up, they might be quite desperate to keep it that way. Confronting them is dangerous. You should leave it to the police." Brandon's brows furrowed as he spoke.

Mud threw his hands in the air. "Come on, Mac. The cops won't do anything on mere speculation."

Brandon let out a long breath. "True," he conceded. "But that doesn't mean you should take the law into your own hands either."

"Talking to someone is not breaking the law." Mud gritted his teeth.

Brandon shook his head. "Whatever, man. Don't say I didn't warn you."

Mud rolled his eyes and saluted. "No worries. Thanks Dad."

Brandon finally relaxed and chuckled. "Please take care of yourself, okay?"

"It's all good, bro. I'm not about to throw myself in harm's way." But he was going to find Andy and Kathleen and confront them with his suspicions.

CHAPTER EIGHTEEN

Amelia ended the phone call and sat on her lounge, chewing on a nail. Brandon had called her to inform her of Mud's crazy plan. Well, potential plan. If she wasn't still seething about him deciding to dump her and go back to Australia, she would be in a panic right now. Who was she kidding? The hurt didn't stop her from caring about him. *Ugh*. Now she was mad *and* anxious.

What was he thinking? Not that she had any idea what to do about it. Her brain was like jelly, much like after the hit-and-run and every other crisis she'd been involved in. She remembered not long before Pa died, he'd had a crazy coughing fit, so bad he was gasping for air. And she'd stood there helplessly for precious minutes, unable to move or think, before she came out of the fog long enough to call 911. They took him to hospital but he never came home again, passing away only a few days later. For years she'd struggled with grief over losing him, guilt over not acting quickly enough, relief that she no longer had to play nurse to him, and guilt again over wanting the respite.

And now, if Mud came to harm and she did nothing to stop him, how would she feel? With trembling fingers she picked up her phone and typed a message to him. That would be something, she supposed. A starting point.

Please don't do anything stupid.

She waited a few minutes before her phone pinged, and by then she'd chewed all her nails down to the quick.

Stupid is how I have behaved toward you these last two months.

Amelia's stomach sank. What? He regretted getting close to her at all? Their whole friendship and romance were stupid? He might as well slice a knife through her heart. Before she took a breath, another message came through.

This might be the one good thing I can do. I want to make this right. Show you what you mean to me.

Amelia's brow furrowed in confusion. Had she read the first message wrong? She scrolled back up and read again. Okay, maybe it wasn't as bad as she first thought. But, still ...

You don't have to put yourself in danger for me.

Would he even listen? She didn't want him to get killed or injured on her behalf. She loved him. Sure, he might choose to move away to the other side of the world, but it didn't change how she felt. And deep down, she'd wondered in the last few days what she was truly angry about. Because the facts were, other than her work with Violet, there was nothing holding her in Trinity Lakes. She had no family here. She didn't even know where her mom was. Her circle of friends was small and she spent precious little time with them. She wasn't even a member of any community club.

So when she'd declared her whole life was in Trinity Lakes, that was a serious overstatement. No, she was more angry that Mud dumped the news on her, rather than opening up and sharing his thoughts and feelings. But, wait, she hadn't been speaking to him in the weeks preceding that conversation. Amelia groaned. She had messed this up as much as Mud had.

I won't be in danger. But you are so worth it.

Amelia's heart flopped over and warmth spread through her body. She sighed. He didn't regret their relationship at all. She still wasn't sure what he deemed wrong about the last two months. Her reaction to his grief and need had been her problem—her mistake—not his. She sent him a couple of love hearts and a "please be careful" message, then shot up a prayer for him.

Amelia sat back in surprise. That might have been the first time she'd ever prayed. True, Violet's words about the love of Jesus had been rolling around in her head for weeks now, and perhaps they'd even worked their way into her heart. She'd softened toward all the God stuff more than she ever had before. Maybe it was time to get off the fence. Maybe it was time to admit she needed someone other than herself, like Mud had admitted. And maybe, if they both learned to lean on God for the big things, they could lean on each other in the day to day.

Amelia closed her eyes. "Lord, if you'll have me. I'm yours. Show me how to live like You want me to." It was a simple prayer but she meant it, and immediately warmth washed over her, as though she'd been embraced. Was this peace? She remained there enjoying that moment for a long time before her phone chimed with a new message.

Hey Meels. Can you come to the police station?

Amelia frowned at the message from Mud, and her stomach churned. *Oh, no.* What had he done?

Right now?

Yes, right now.

Amelia chewed her lip. Wasn't she supposed to be mad at him? But after the last couple hours, that all seemed to have faded away and quiet assurance had taken its place. She glanced at the time. Oh, it was past dinnertime and she hadn't even noticed she was hungry. No time for food now. Mud's message sounded urgent. She grabbed her purse and keys and typed Mud another message.

On my way.

By the time she got to the station, nerves had set in. What had happened? They hadn't even sorted through his declaration after the wedding yet. Would he now expect her to bail him out or something? Amelia drew in a deep breath and pushed through the door, searching the room for any familiar face. Where was Mud? A female trooper noticed her and waved her over to the counter.

"Are you Ms. Jones?"

"Yes." Amelia hesitated.

"Come through." She waved Amelia toward a door then came around with her security key to give her access. Amelia ducked inside and was shown to an interview room. Seated at the table was none other than Mud with Sheriff Thompson. She glanced at his wrists. No cuffs. Relief flooded through her. What then?

"Hey." She sat on the spare chair, more than a little breathless.

"Hey, yourself." Mud smiled.

"Good news, Ms. Jones," Sheriff Thompson said.

Amelia's eyes swerved to the sheriff. "What happened?"

"Mr. Murchison here somehow convinced your hit-and-run driver to turn themselves in." His stern gaze shifted to Mud. "Once again, son, inadvisable. You might have found yourself in a world of trouble."

Amelia stared at one then the other. Obviously they'd been talking for a while, and she guessed the sheriff had reamed Mud for his part. But her mind returned to the other statement the sheriff had made. "He turned himself in?"

"Correct." Sheriff Thompson jerked his chin down. "They are being questioned in another room as we speak."

"They?" Amelia's eyes swerved between the two again.

"Andy and Kathleen," Mud told her, immediately receiving a glare from the sheriff, which made him press his lips together and sit back in silence.

The sheriff placed two photos in front of Amelia.

"Do you recognize either of these people?" Sheriff Thompson asked.

Amelia looked at the photos, then up at the sheriff and back again. "I mean, I've seen pictures of Andy O'Dell on the computer, but I've never met him. As for the girl," she shook her head. "No, I've never seen her."

The sheriff laid out a third image. "Do you recognize this vehicle?"

The YODELL license plate stood out to her as it had the first, and second, time she saw it. "Yes. That's the car involved in the hit-and-run, as I've told you before."

"Thank you." The sheriff gathered up the photos. "I just needed confirmation."

"What happened?"

Sheriff Thompson paused and tapped the corner of his file on the desk as if considering his next words. "I'll let your boyfriend tell you all about it. Even though it was risky, his actions have brought this case to a satisfactory close." He turned to Mud again. "I hope I never have to see you in here again. And I mean that in the nicest possible way."

"Thank you, sir." Mud nodded, clearly trying to hold back a grin.

As the sheriff held the door open for them, Mud steered

her out with a gentle hand on her lower back. "Can we go to Joe's Diner? I'm starved and I have heaps to tell you."

Amelia remembered her empty stomach. "Sure. Meet you there."

———

MUD ARRIVED at Joe's before Amelia and he found a booth in the back. He smiled to himself as he scanned the menu and called the server over.

Five minutes later he saw her at the door, searching, and he waved to get her attention. She strode over, her gaze everywhere except on him, then slid into the booth opposite.

"Thanks for coming, Meels. I've already ordered for you. Your favorite."

She lifted her eyebrows at him.

"Bacon and cheese burger, right?" His mouth quirked up at the side. "I've eaten with you enough to notice."

"With—"

"Double the cheese and bacon. Yep. And I also got you an iced mocha."

Now he probably looked smug. But he wanted her to know he noticed all the little details about her. That he wasn't in this just to gratify his ego or take her for granted.

"Well done." Amelia's lips twitched, but she didn't let out a proper smile. "So, spill. What did you do? How did you get them to confess?"

"Well, I drove around there and waited until Kathleen turned up."

"How did you know she would?" Amelia interrupted.

"I didn't. I hoped. But I was in luck. I knew what she looked like from her socials online, so when she went into his house, I went and knocked on the door."

"Just like that." Amelia's eyes widened. "You walked up to their front door. Did you even have a plan?"

Mud shifted in his seat. It was all a bit hare-brained now that he looked back. "Not really. I kind of prayed for God to help me, but that's it."

"No wonder the sheriff was mad at you."

"Yeah." Mud swallowed his chagrin. "Anyway, I introduced myself and basically told them our suspicions."

"No pussyfooting around with you, is there?"

Mud chuckled. She was probably referring to more than him speaking to YODELL. "I guess not. But when I told them my theory, they looked guilty as. I reckon I hit the nail on the head. I told them I thought Kathleen was driving and Andy was protecting her, then I asked her if she even had a current driver's license."

Mud paused as their food arrived. After thanking the server, he continued.

"Next thing, Kathleen starts crying. I guess the guilt was too much. She tells me she lost her license three months ago. Yes, she'd borrowed YODELL's car. She didn't see the pedestrian lights in time, and when she hit the boy and the dog, she panicked and drove off. O'Dell raved on about how he loves her and doesn't want her to go to jail, so they covered it all up."

Amelia's mouth hung open. "Oh, my goodness. For real?"

Mud nodded, took a bite from his burger and waited to swallow before he answered. "Yep. But Kathleen begged me to keep it quiet. I had to remind her it nearly cost a boy his life and his beloved dog was gone forever, and how could they deny that family the truth and closure?

"In the end, I think I swayed Andy more than Kathleen, and he promised to come clean and agreed to go with me to the cop shop. He pretty much had to carry Kathleen to the car, though." Mud popped a crispy chip into his mouth.

"So what will happen to them?" Amelia asked. "I mean, it's kind of sad in a way. Will Kathleen go to prison?"

Mud shrugged as he ate another of his fries. "I am happy to leave that to the justice system. It's a pretty serious offence. Neither of them will come out of this with zero consequences."

"Hmm." Amelia sipped at her drink looking thoughtful, perhaps even wistful.

"Aren't you happy to have closure on this?" She didn't respond the way he thought she might.

She put her glass down. "Of course I am. But it's a little bitter-sweet hearing the true story behind it. It would have been easier if it were some heartless drunk."

Mud pushed his plate away from him. "Sure. I suppose so. But she knew what she was doing when she drove without a license in the first place."

Amelia reached out a hand and clasped his. He glanced up to see gratitude in her eyes. "I'm sorry. I sound ungrateful. I do appreciate that you wanted to find out the truth for me."

The tension in his stomach dispersed at her touch and at her words. He covered her hand with his free one. "Yeah, it was only for you."

Their eyes locked for a moment and he saw a million thoughts racing through her mind before she landed on something to say. "I'm sorry I stormed off the other night." Her eyes dipped to the table. "It was … it was a bit of a shock to suddenly hear you say you're going back to Australia. I wasn't ready for that."

Mud squeezed her hand. "Hey, I shouldn't have dumped it on you like that." He drew in a deep breath. "I've never been good at this dating thing. Not in a serious way anyhow."

"What do you mean, Mud?" Her throat convulsed as she swallowed. "You make me feel like I'm the only woman on the planet when I'm with you. I've never experienced that before."

"That's because you *are* the only woman on earth when we're together." He shook his head and released her hand. "But I've come on really strong, haven't I, and never made you any promises?"

Amelia sat back a little and gripped the edge of the table with both hands. "Oh."

"So I understand why you were upset with me. I raised your hopes for a future without intending to."

"Oh," she said again, as her eyes became glassy. "Are you breaking up with me?"

What? How did she come to that? Mud rubbed his hands over his face. "No, that's not what I meant. I'm trying to say sorry for leading you on when I wasn't ready to commit. I should have kept things more ... platonic back then."

A small creased appeared between her brows. "And now?"

Ugh. He was messing this up right royally. *You love her. Tell her you love her.* The words stuck in his throat, and he coughed. Not tonight. He couldn't do it tonight. "Can we try again? How about I take you out on a special date tomorrow night?"

Amelia hesitated, obviously still confused by his rambling. "I'd love to go out with you, Mud, but—"

"Tomorrow night," he interrupted. "Tomorrow night I'll be better. Clearer. Okay?"

"Okay." She still sounded wary.

"I'll pick you up at seven."

"I'll be waiting."

CHAPTER NINETEEN

True to his word, Mud turned up right on seven o'clock, and as Amelia had promised, she was ready and waiting for him. He'd given her no clue where he was taking her, so she dressed somewhere between casual and fancy, and hoped that would suffice.

Mud came to the door and she breathed out relief when she saw he wore jeans and a button-down shirt. He leaned in and kissed her on the cheek, filling her senses with cologne, and her mouth went dry.

"You look great," she stammered. The navy with charcoal undertones of his shirt set off his sun-browned skin to perfection, and the slim fit showed off his powerful physique.

"And you are drop-dead gorgeous." He took her hand and led her to his car. The butterflies within multiplied at his words. But the fact his car was a rental reminded her he would leave the country soon.

Should she tell him her thoughts about that had changed in the last couple days? Amelia chewed on her lip as they drove. Maybe later. She would enjoy their date first and talk seriously after. And from where he parked, she guessed they were going to the theater.

"What's showing tonight?" Amelia asked.

The corner of Mud's mouth curved up as he drove into a parking space. "*My Fair Lady.*"

Amelia clapped her hands. "Oh, I love the old classics."

"Thought you might appreciate it." Mud took her arm as they headed into the retro theater.

They headed to the counter and found Linyu Foo serving. "Hey, Foo," Amelia greeted.

"Oh, hey. Great to see you two here again." Foo kept working as he spoke. "Audrey Hepburn can never disappoint."

"Absolutely not," Amelia agreed.

Mud standing behind her, leaned close to whisper in her ear. "She doesn't hold a candle to you, though."

Heat rose in her cheeks. She hoped her face didn't color along with it. She turned and threw him a fake frown. "Stop it."

"What?" Mud feigned innocence.

Foo's glance swerved to Mud and back to Amelia again and a slow, knowing smile appeared on his face. "What can I get you?"

Mud stepped forward, sliding an arm around Amelia's waist. "The works. Tickets. Popcorn. Drinks. Chocolate—"

"He means candy," Amelia cut in, too aware of his nearness.

"Yeah, candy," Mud confirmed. "And ice cream. Don't forget ice cream."

"Coming right up." Foo's grin spread even wider.

Soon, Amelia and Mud had their arms laden with treats and headed to the cinema.

"Enjoy the movie," Foo called after them.

They found seats near the back in the middle, her favorite place to sit.

While the ads ran on the screen, Mud turned to her. "Can I ask you a question?"

Amelia removed the straw from her mouth and put her drink in the cupholder. "Shoot."

His face became serious. "Before I turned up and started, you know, hanging around you, um …"

"Courting me?" Amelia supplied. *Sweeping me off my feet. Upending my world.* They were terms she'd never say aloud.

"Yeah, that." He looked sheepish. "Before then, what did your future look like? I mean, what plans did you have?"

Amelia thought back to the world before Mud, before he first showed up last year. The sworn off all men, determined to be an independent woman for the rest of her life version of herself. No, that's not the answer she would give him, because it was born out of hurt. She picked up her drink and fiddled with the straw. "I wanted to have a family and settle down, I guess, like most people." Amelia couldn't bring herself to tell him how much she wanted to be loved—properly loved—mutually supportive, doing-life-together kind of love.

"And what about career-wise?"

"Well, I studied for my MBA, but I started working with Violet. I use my business skills with the Reynolds Group, but I've never thought beyond that because I enjoy it so much. I mean, working for your best friend has its benefits, you know?"

"Yeah, I get that."

Amelia figured he probably did understand that, since he'd worked with Nick on and off on different projects over the years. Never permanently, though. Glancing at her watch, she realized the movie was about to start. "Hey, I'm gonna run to the bathroom real quick. I don't want to miss anything once the movie's underway."

———

MUD FINISHED his ice cream and found a napkin to wipe the sticky mess from his fingers. He should've asked Amelia those questions weeks ago. He was impressed that she had completed a degree after what she'd endured with her father. Although she was forced to learn independence, it created a strength of character in her she may not have had otherwise. He wondered if she ever saw it that way.

She was happy in her occupation, which was great. Many people never found satisfaction with their work. Himself, for example. But hopefully he would find that contentment in nursing. For Amelia, though, it would be a lot to ask her to step away from Violet and start something entirely new in Australia. All of this required some re-thinking.

As he sat and waited for Amelia to return, a familiar smell drifted to his nose. A smell that made his stomach clench and sweat bead on his forehead.

Smoke.

Mud closed his eyes as his heartbeat ratcheted up. It was probably someone sneaking a cigarette in the theater. He tried to focus on his breathing. In and out, slowly. In and out.

Except it didn't smell like cigarette smoke. Mud raised his gaze to the ceiling and clenched his hands into fists, punching them into his thighs. *Stop panicking. It's probably nothing.* The fire sprinkler heads hadn't come on. Was he too premature in thinking a fire was in progress?

But he couldn't sit there waiting to find out if a fire was ablaze. He needed to find the source of the smell. Before he'd even moved out of the row, a siren's wail filled the theater and water began to spray from the roof. Someone had activated the fire alarm.

What? Now? Here? And where was Amelia?

He wanted to run, escape, but all his instincts kicked in with a rush of adrenaline. He needed to find Amelia, but he also needed to make sure everyone got out of this cinema. Instead of heading to the exit, he ran to the front and herded everyone out.

"Stay calm. Just walk." He touched the shoulder of someone who remained seated. "Please, sir, you need to evacuate. There is a fire in the building."

Hopefully, Amelia was in a safe place, perhaps already outside on the street. *Please God.* And the sooner he saw this cinema empty the sooner he could locate her.

When the last person left, he quickly returned and double-checked, bending down to look beneath seats in case someone hid there. The smoke thickened now despite the rain of water, and he saw the gray haze in the light of the projected film, which continued to run on the screen. Mud ripped his shirt open and pulled his t-shirt up to cover his mouth and nose, then crouched down to stay beneath the acrid smoke as he headed for the exit.

Mud stayed behind the crowd as they all exited the building and spilled out onto the street. Once free of the front doors, he frantically searched for Amelia among all the people milling around. He couldn't see her anywhere. His heart pumped even harder and, in his panic, he started yelling her name. *Please, God, where is she?*

He spotted Linyu Foo standing to the side with two of his employees gathered, arms around each other's shoulders. "Foo," he called as he approached. He lifted a pale and distraught face. "Have you seen Amelia?"

NEVER SAY YOU NEED ME

"No." He shook his head, and his shoulders shook with unshed tears. "I thought everyone was out."

"She went to the bathroom. Did anyone check there?"

One employee, white faced, turned to him. "We couldn't get there. The fire was down the hall near the amenities."

Foo crumpled to the pavement. A perfect picture of what was happening in Mud's mind. She was still in there? His beautiful Amelia. He should have told her he loved her. Was it too late to ever have the chance?

Sirens wailed in the distance. The firetrucks were on their way.

———

AMELIA HUDDLED in the corner of the ladies' room, unable to move, unable to scream, unable to even think clearly. She'd been finishing up when the fire alarm sounded and she froze, her mind going to that foggy place it always did in emergencies.

By the time she'd gathered her senses to make a run for it, smoke seeped beneath the door, making her panic all the more. She'd retreated from the door until her back connected with the opposite wall. She slid down to the ground, her breath coming rapidly, and whimpered prayers for Jesus to help her.

Somewhere amidst the abstract thoughts that flitted through her mind, Mud's face appeared in her memory. Trying to grasp the intangible, she called out his name. "Mud."

Over and over she called him, but breathing in deeply to get any volume out made her cough violently as her lungs filled with smoke. She was going to die. She was going to die here, alone, without Mud ever knowing she would cross the world for him.

Orange light flickered beneath the bathroom door opposite her. The fire must be getting closer. Did anyone even know she was in here?

Her phone. She felt all her pockets and almost cried. She'd left it with Mud when she ducked to the bathroom.

As desperation overrode her brain-fog, Amelia scrambled to her feet. There must be a window she could smash to escape. *Please Jesus, save me.* In the haze of suffocating smoke, she felt and searched along what she hoped was an external wall, often halting to cough again as the poisoned air chafed her lungs. But no, not a single window existed, except those vents up near the roof. And they were far too small for a person to climb through.

No way out. She was stuck. Doomed.

She choked on the smoke, and sank to the floor once again, lying down on the smooth tiles to cry and cough ... and pray.

———

MUD STOOD bent over with his hands on his knees, knowing in his gut he had to do something. The trucks wouldn't arrive in time. Even now, Amelia might be dying in there. Fear ripped at every nerve in his body at the thought of entering the burning building, flashes of that house last summer in Australia searing his mind. He didn't want to face that again. And yet he refused to stand by and do nothing.

He sucked in several deep breaths, then approached an employee he'd seen with a fire blanket around their shoulders.

"May I borrow this, please?" He fought to keep his voice steady.

The teen shrugged. "I guess I don't need it anymore." She handed it over.

Mud swung the blanket around his shoulders and strode purposefully toward the door.

"Wait," someone yelled.

"Don't go in there." Another voice.

"Stop. You'll get yourself killed." Yet another.

Mud ignored them all and pushed through the swinging doors. Billowing smoke filled the foyer, and he saw the blaze of flames down the hallway to his right, sprinklers doing little to slow the burn. That must be where the ladies' room was. Terror gripped him as he prepared to run into the flames, but it was now or never. He pulled the blanket tight and charged toward the fire with a roar.

He was thankful to find enough space between the flames and the door of the bathroom to access it, and he smashed the door open without hesitation. There she was on the floor at the far end.

"Amelia." He bolted to her and kneeled down, patting her face. "Meels. Milly. Come on, talk to me."

No response.

Mud gritted his teeth. There was no time to assess her further. He needed to get her out of there. Without waiting another second, he wrapped her in the fire blanket and hoisted her over his shoulder. Out the door, he skirted the encroaching inferno and made a run for it to the main exit.

Safely outside, he gently lowered his precious burden to the ground as firefighters swarmed past him to combat the blaze. He reached to check her pulse, but was elbowed away by a paramedic.

"We'll take over now, thanks."

"But she's my—" A fit of coughing consumed him then, leaving him unable to finish. *She's my girl,* his head screamed.

Another paramedic took one look at him and tugged him away to the ambulance. "We need to check you over as well."

Mud tried to fight them off but he couldn't breathe, couldn't even speak. And all he wanted was to know if Amelia would be okay.

———

AMELIA FLOATED in a calming sea of nothingness. All was still and peaceful except for an annoying beep that kept recurring, intruding on her rest. She wished it would go away, and she groaned.

Next thing, a hand covered hers and a familiar, though raspy, voice spoke. "Meels? Are you awake?"

She opened her eyes, blinked, then squinted against the bright lights. "Where am I?" Her voice sounded weird, and she lifted her free hand to touch her face, only to find a mask over her mouth.

"It's okay." Mud readjusted the mask. "You're in the hospital. This is for oxygen."

Amelia closed her eyes. Tried to remember. Oh. "There was a fire." She swallowed against the roughness in her throat.

"Yeah, but we got you out in time." Mud's face curved in a grim smile, still squeezing her hand.

"I thought I was going to die." Tears slid from the corners of her eyes as memories assailed her.

Mud released her hand, instead brushing the tears from her face with a gentle caress of his thumb. "It's okay. It's all over now."

"What happened?"

Mud pressed his lips into a thin line and sighed. "Sounds like it was arson. Someone deliberately set fire to the cinema. Can you believe it?"

"Is Foo alright?"

Mud stroked her cheek again. "Look at you, always worrying about the other person. He's fine. Devastated about the fire. Grateful no one was seriously hurt. Thankful the firies put it out before it jumped to neighboring businesses. But it will take him a long while to recover and rebuild from the damage to the theater, even with insurance."

"What's wrong with your voice?" He sounded so gravelly.

"Smoke inhalation," he said simply. "Just not as bad as you."

"Oh," she said as understanding hit. "You were the one who saved me?"

His face lit in a lopsided grin. "As if I'd let anyone else do it."

Tears welled again. "You risked your life for me?"

Mud rolled his eyes. "I've told you before, you're worth it."

Amelia tried to sit up and Mud helped her, plumping pillows behind her. "When can I get out of here?"

Mud's eyes traveled to the door and back to her. "Well, you were unconscious when I found you. They said you weren't breathing, but with oxygen they got you back. The doctor will tell you properly, but they cleared your lungs out and now they're monitoring you to make sure your oxygen levels stay healthy."

"And you?" she asked. "Are you okay?"

Mud chuckled. "You can't keep me down long. I needed oxygen, too, but I'm fine now."

"I bet Sheriff Thompson's not happy with you, though." Amelia giggled inside her mask, then coughed.

"You should have seen the look on his face when he came to take my statement." Mud winked at her. "I reckon he's ready to have me deported."

That word sobered her. "Mud. We ..."

"Shhh." He placed a finger over her lips. "That can wait. The minute you're discharged, we're going to finish our date."

"I don't think the theater will be up to screening movies for a while." Amelia shuddered, even though she tried to make her words light.

Mud gave a wry smile. "What? You don't want to sit among the ashes? It might be a new trend."

Amelia shook her head. "The only ashes I want to see in future, are in a campfire or open fireplace at home."

He laughed. "I one hundred percent agree with you there."

CHAPTER TWENTY

Mud and Amelia strolled hand in hand along the path beside Lake Wainscott enjoying the summer evening. They fell into easy conversation about their newfound faith experiences. Apart from a sore throat, Amelia felt great. It seemed crazy that she'd come so close to death, but was thankful she had the chance to really live again.

As Mud had promised, he picked her up from the hospital and drove her to her unit to shower and dress in the comfort of her own home. Then he took her straight out to dinner, followed by this visit to the lake.

"Did you have one of those NDEs?" Mud asked her as they ambled along the lakefront.

Amelia lifted a shoulder. "No. No near-death experience. The last thing I remember is being on the floor in the bathroom, and the next I woke up with you sitting beside me." She squeezed his hand and offered him a grateful smile. And she *was* grateful. With Violet in the Canadian mountains and thus out of contact, Mud was the only person around who stayed by her. Sure, Breanna and Lucy both dropped by to check on her, and Foo came in with a big bouquet. But Mud had been there every minute the doctors allowed him.

"But I can tell you this," she added. "After that experience, I want to make the most of life. Not waste any more time. Does that make sense?"

Mud pressed his lips into a half smile. "Completely. I felt the same after Griff died. I needed to find purpose. Meaning."

He sat down on a bench seat by the path and tugged her down to join him, slipping an arm around her shoulders.

"Do you think you've found that now?" Amelia rested against him.

"Yeah." Mud's voice sounded wistful. "Partly with discovering Jesus as my Savior, partly with this conviction to become a nurse." He paused and his throat convulsed behind Amelia's cheek as he swallowed. "And partly with you."

Amelia sat straighter and turned to him, a question forming on her lips, but he continued.

"I've never met anyone like you, Meels." He took both her hands in his. "In a few short months, you've become my best friend. You make me want to be a better man. And more than that, I love you. Head to toe, I am deeply, forever, yours." He let out a wobbly laugh. "If you want me, of course."

What words could she say that would even come close? Instead, she threw her arms around his neck and kissed him hard. When she finally pulled back she found the only words that would suffice. "I love you, too."

Mud released a shaky breath. "I'm so glad to hear that. You have no idea." He shook his head, but his face was aglow with what might be called awe. He captured her hands again. "We need to talk about the future, though."

"Yes, we do." Amelia agreed. They needed to sort out how they would navigate a relationship with two different countries involved.

"I've made a decision," Mud began. "I should never have asked you to give up everything and come to Australia with me. That was selfish. But, since I can't imagine my life without you either, I will make the move here."

Amelia gaped at him. "You would do that? For me?" No one had ever made such a sacrifice for her, choosing her and her wishes over everything else.

"I've told you at least a hundred times." Mud rolled his eyes. "You're worth it."

"But what about your family?"

Mud shrugged. "I'm not sure. I suppose Mum and Dad can move here, too. But that's something we can figure out later. Somehow, God can handle it."

Amelia stared at him in amazement. How did she find such an exceptional man? It was time to make a confession, but she couldn't keep the smile from spreading on her face. "I've made a decision too."

"Oh yeah? What's that?" Mud grinned back at her.

"I realized the other day that there is really nothing keeping me here. I'm moving to Austra—"

Mud's lips stopped her mouth, and his arms wound around her waist, pulling tight. And then she knew it, like she'd never known it before. She belonged to this man. They belonged together. If he needed her, she would be there for him, and if she needed him, likewise, he would be there for her. The mutually giving relationship she'd always dreamed of was now a reality that made her heart sing as she kissed him with all the love she had.

"You know this means you have to marry me, right?"

Mud whispered against her lips when they finally came up for air.

There was no hiding her smile this time. "Absolutely."

THE END

AUTHOR'S NOTE

Thank you for reading *Never Say You Need Me*. It was an honor to be included in the Trinity Lakes Series alongside some of my favorite authors. It was a step outside my usual genre of historical romance, but I loved every minute of it.

If you enjoyed this story, would you mind taking the time to put a review on the site where you purchased it, or on the Goodreads website? All reviews are helpful for authors to widen their reader base, and your support is always appreciated.

Thank you again. Until next time.

Amanda.

ACKNOWLEDGEMENTS

I would like to offer special thanks to Drew O'Hare, Kathleen Harrison and Philip Foo for their significant contributions to Reveal Church Global Missions in return for having their names in this novel. Your generosity is much appreciated.

NEXT IN TRINITY LAKES ROMANCE SERIES

Always On My Mind
Book #19

by Iola Goulton

Who are you if you can't remember who you are?

Tiffany Thomas has spent the last five years treading water, unable to move past her unforgivable mistake, redeem herself, and find peace.

After she rescues a mystery man from a canoeing accident, assisting with his recovery is another opportunity for her to make good and move on. Ryan Jordan has lost his memory. The information in his wallet gives him the basics, but not what counts: his true character. There's a photo of him with a woman and two children. His family? If so, where are they, and why is he alone in Trinity Lakes? Tiffany joins Ryan in his quest to find himself. Spending time with Ryan challenges her to find the truth in her own life, even as she fights her growing attraction to him. But can she ever accept God's truth and forgive herself? A small-town contemporary Christian billionaire romance. Welcome to Trinity Lakes, a warm and welcoming small town in east Washington, filled with charm, family, and friends, where fresh starts, second chances, and romance abound. You'll meet swoony bachelors, cowboys, and adventurers, sweet and sassy ladies, and your new best friends. This series of standalone Christian romances will warm your heart, inspire your faith, and bring a smile to your soul.

ABOUT THE AUTHOR

Amanda Deed is an award-winning author residing in Melbourne with her husband, her grown-up children, and several birds. Outside of her family, her life revolves around words, numbers (writing and accounting) and a healthy splash of music.

Her first novel, *The Game*, won the 2010 CALEB Prize for Fiction, and she has since had several novels final in the same prize. Amanda loves to write novels that explore her faith, Australian history, and romance.

For more information, and to subscribe to her newsletter, go to www.amandadeed.com.

ALSO BY AMANDA DEED

Trinity Lakes Romance

Blue Skies Dreaming

Stand Alone Titles

The Game

Relentless

Jackson's Creek Trilogy

Ellenvale Gold

Black Forest Redemption

Henry's Run

Fractured Fairy Tales

Unnoticed

Unhinged

The Captive's Song

The Greenfield Legacy